Hunter's Mark

A Novella

By

Joseph E Koob II

D1518402

Prequel to

The Making of a Bard Book I

of

The Chronicles of Borea

The Chronicles of Borea

Seven-Book Fantasy Series

ISBN: 979-8-847-68125-4

About the Author

Dr. Koob is a former college music educator, having taught: – Music Appreciation; Music History Course Sequence; Private and class Stringed Instruments –Violin, Viola, Cello, Bass; Music Education and Student Teacher Supervisor; Student Success classes; Interdisciplinary advanced seminars; and Music Theory. He also conducted University-Civic Symphonies for many years and has performed in symphony orchestras in the United States and Europe.

Dr. Koob served in the United States Air Force during Vietnam as a C-141 Starlifter Navigator.

His educational background includes: Bachelor of Music – DePauw University; Master's Degree in Violin – Montclair State University; Master's in Counseling, Northern State University; and Doctorate in Education – University of Illinois.

Writing Awards: *A Perfect Day – Guide for a Better Life:* ***Winner – Best Book Non-fiction,*** Oklahoma Writers Federation, and ***Honorable Mention,*** *Writer's Digest* Self-Published Book Awards. Winner Various Local and Regional Writing Competitions

His background includes work as an Executive Coach and Motivational Speaker; Author of Music Educational Software, Music Texts, Manuals, and Adjudicated Articles; and many books and articles on "Understanding and Working with Difficult People." He has many additional interests, including bicycling, woodworking, painting, reading, archery hunting, fishing, and more. Joe is happily married and has two grown children. He divides his time between FL and MI.

Acknowledgements

Much thanks to everyone who has influenced me over the years.

Thanks to: my wife, Lisa; my children, Nathan and Elise, and Pat, son-in-law, who have been readers throughout the development of this series and helped me in innumerable supportive ways with this project; Anne Duston, one of my regular readers; Carolyn K.; as well as other readers and friends. Special thanks to my good friend and expert editor, Steve Bridge, who set me on the path to righteousness early on in this process, and who has been instrumental in making the final editions so much better. Thanks also to Stephanie H. of SLL Editorial Services for her early editing; Phil Lang for his work on the cover; and my cousin, Robert Haselier, for his wonderful illustrations and cover art.

Website: **chroniclesofborea.com:** offers additional information for readers as well as announcements of Book Releases and other items that might be of interest.

Blog: chroniclesofboreabooks.wordpress.com

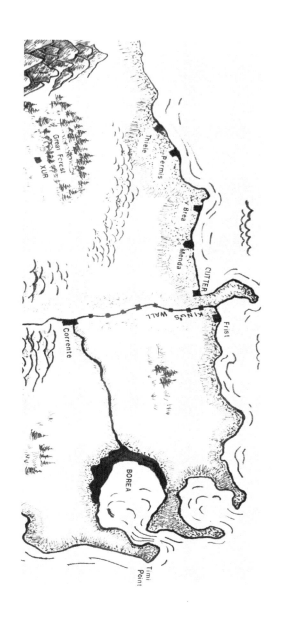

North Coast of Borea

Contents

Waning Moon

The forest is rarely a quiet place. And near dusk, on a late winter day, it can be a remarkable blend of unusual sounds. A vole tunneling in and under the vestiges of ice crystals that have melted and frozen numerous times sounds curiously like bacon popping on a highly heated cast iron grill. A squirrel scrambling up a dead conifer, scraping across the dried remnants that often crumble under its sharp claws, can mimic a village carpenter shaving the bark off a tree with a draw knife. Three pregnant does moving across the dried fall leaves on the forest floor scuff their hooves just enough to let the other woodland creatures know that the coming spring will bring new life. The wind creates a backdrop of gentle sounds that speak to the movement of anything no longer attached as they float about the contours of the land itself.

But...

Here. Now. The forest is quiet.

Near dusk, today, there is no wind.

The vole, afraid of its own shadow, is frozen in place, waiting.

The deer have scattered, for they know that danger lurks.

The half-elven hunter, standing behind a tall pine, would normally have heard all of these sounds and more. Since he has been there for several hours, quietly, patiently waiting, he has become part of the stillness. He is knowledgeable enough about the lore of the forest to have prepared his spot carefully – brushing away anything within ten feet of the roots of the tree, so that he could shift his position, step over to another pine, or ready his weapon without making any sound at all. Or at least any sound that could be heard by the forest creatures that might normally be active this time of day.

No, he is not the cause of the quietude. It is something else.

Picking his hunting location, downwind for the afternoon wait, the hunter carefully cut away any branch that he might brush against when readying his bow. He has also prepared his stand, by judiciously pruning the thickets that abut the paths along which his prey might pass, as well as along the line-of-sight of his chosen shooting lane. His bow, made by his own hand, is of layered yew, horn, and sinew construction. Strong, flexible, forty inches in length, it was designed to be powerful enough to kill at up to a hundred paces, though a good hunter would rarely shoot over thirty to ensure a clean death. Its short length allows him to move in a confined space and easily adjust his position and aim, should his prey alter its course. He is an exceptional shot.

For his youthful appearance, the half-elf is well-trained. Like the vole, he waits now, without moving, in anticipation of the stealthy, deadly creature's approach.

It moves silently. One step – the paw lifted and placed lightly on the chosen path. A glance, right, downwind, then left, upwind. Another step. The cat is cognizant of everything, anything, within range of its sight and hearing along its route. An extra sense, long practiced, often tells him that something near might actually be able to do him harm. Another stop, wait, sharply alert with all his senses – then a step, and another, checking again. Softly moving on pine needles, avoiding the scattered leaves of the hardwoods that would surely give him away, his body flows gracefully. Stopping, checking again. Making sure. Another step.

Though he is hungry, he does not let that drive him from his path. Soon enough, when it is nearing full dark, he will eat. His prey will be unable to escape once he leaps from cover.

The hunter, though, has prepared carefully as well. Above all, he too has learned patience. And he has also learned grace in movement, though it did not come as naturally as it did for the prey that he is waiting to engage. His clothing has been chosen and checked so that he can move as quietly as any creature he might hunt. His camouflage is from the environ that he hunts, and it has been reinforced this day by selected branches, leaves, pine needles, and shrubs that are placed to enhance his concealment. More than anything, the lad has learned from years of experience what he could expect from the forest, from himself, and from the creatures he hunts.

The big cat takes another step, his soft paw coming to rest with the tiniest part of its edge on a small mound of crystalized snow… that shifts.

The hunter hears.

He slowly brings his right foot, encased in a boot of the softest of leather, up off the cleared ground, placing it forty-degrees to the right of its former position. He shifts his weight gently onto that leg as he eases his bow up, also to the right, ever so slowly. So slowly, that someone or something would need to be looking directly at the darkened wood to see that it has shifted in his grasp and is coming up.

With his arrow already nocked, the hunter begins to draw back, but only until he feels enough tension on the string that the arrow will not slip its position. He waits again.

The mountain lion has not moved since his last slight mis-step. Nor has it heard or sensed anything. Yet still it pauses.

Finally, the deadly cat shifts its weight forward and slowly lifts its opposite front leg for another step. This makes no sound, but the hunter sees – a movement from the direction of the sound he had heard moments before. For he has not only excellent hearing, but the exceptional sight of the half-elven.

Time is becoming a factor. The forest is darkening.

The lion is mostly hidden behind a dense shrub, with only the lighter, front part of its snout and the barest outline of its right front paw visible to the hunter. Though the boy could guess the location for a killing shot through the thicket, his planned shooting lane is several feet to the right. He will not move again until the cat has come further out, farther into his prepared opening. It would be foolish to try any other shot. A tiny twig of two inches can deflect a shaft, no matter how well aimed. The waiting will continue; he only hopes the cat will step ahead far enough before the light fades too much for an accurate and honorable shot.

Finally, another step. So quiet and graceful that the hunter would not have bet on the movement. But he sees. Another step, and he catches a shift of the white muzzle. He is sure.

The mountain lion is hungrier now, and the fat sheep below in the pasture are tempting him to be incautious – another step, and another. The cat glances right, left, its extra sense, now dulled by the emptiness of its stomach. A fatal mistake.

The hunter raises his bow the final few inches to eye level as the lion looks left again, away from where the hunter stands, ready now. The lad has a split second to draw back and then... to wait again.

Holding at full draw is something also practiced, his father drilling him and his brother over and over. "Learn to shoot quickly, because your life might depend on it; but also, learn to hold on target – for minutes if necessary – to make sure you have the best shot," Manfred had exhorted them.

The cat pauses again; something has changed, but the cat isn't sure what it is. It doesn't finish its last step, instead staying low, remaining in a slight crouch, readying for a leap away if it senses anything at all. Sniffing the air, though there was virtually no breeze, the cat waits again.

Sweat trickles down the lad's neck and nose; he doesn't flinch. Steady, steady, he thinks...

Now!

The mountain lion had turned its head once more to the left – to be sure nothing had changed. It was its last mistake. As the cat moved its right leg ahead, the boy released, sending the arrow flying through the tunnel he had created in the brush, straight and true. A loud "Thwack" resounded through the quiet as the ultra-sharp blade struck, penetrating the lung and heart before exiting the far side, behind the left leg. The mountain lion leapt, up and forward, in its dying effort to be away; but it ended diving headfirst into the pine straw on the side of the path it had been following. Its top front leg twitched. The cat lay still.

The half-elven lad waited, watching. Five minutes... ten... the large cat did not move.

From his position, Jared could see it was big, probably the biggest cat he had seen – fully twelve or more stone weight. Thankfully, his brother would help with the drag.

After counting off fifteen minutes, he stepped onto the path he and Ge-or** had scouted for almost a week – so as to be sure of how the mountain lion travelled from up in the steep hills down to the village's pastureland in search of sheep. A big mountain lion could devastate a flock, and sometimes it would even take a small cow. This one had been on the rampage for months during the hard winter. The brothers, known for their forestry skills, as well as their prowess with their bows, would earn five silver for their efforts, money that would be useful this spring – their mother suffering from a long winter illness.

**Considering the unique linguistic characteristics of Old Borean, and Ge-or's heritage, historians have agreed that his name would have been pronounced "Gay-or" in contrast to the current popular vernacular "Gee-or" or the more vulgar "George."

Jared whistled loudly, thrice. The signal for his brother to descend from his blocking, back-up position on the hill to his right. He yelled, "Ge-or, to me."

Sidling carefully up to the body of the mountain lion, Jared first poked it with the tip of his bow, assuring that the cat was dead. He then knelt next to it; and placing his hand on its forehead, he whispered an ancient prayer to the old Gods, thanking them and the cat for this gift. Though the people of the North Coast rarely hunted big cats for food, the meat this spring would be welcome, divided by the village's poor. He and Ge-or would cape out the skin and gift it to their mother, who would find good use for it.

While gutting the animal, Jared's brother arrived. "A fine animal, Jared. Have you blessed him?"

Jared nodded. Then, without speaking, he stood. Ritualistically bowing to the cat and then his brother, he followed this simple ceremony by raising his bloody forefinger and drawing a crude arrow on Ge-or's forehead.

Ge-or wet his finger in the animal's blood, too, marking Jared in a similar way. The hunter's mark, it was called. Typically a simple smear with one's thumb or finger on the forehead of the hunter who had taken the animal, the two boys had chosen to individualize their hunts, as well as honor each other, with this symbol. Though Jared had brought the cat down, they both had been instrumental in parts of the hunt. Their mark was to acknowledge the new life they had taken, for neither lad had ever killed one of the great mountain lions before, though each had taken other forest cats. Mountain lions were rare creatures in the north country these days. Qa-ryks and other evil beasts had killed most and driven the others to the south.

Jared proceeded with carefully removing the animal's entrails. Much could be saved. There was no sense in spoiling any of the meat by careless cutting. After taking out the organ meats, and setting aside those that could be used, he wiped the chest cavity with fresh pine needles from nearby trees, cleaning it carefully of blood. Then, the gutting done, heart, liver, and other organs placed carefully in the gut cavity with fresh snow to cool the offal, Jared tied the cat's legs together in order to keep the organs in place during the drag to their camp. After all was ready, Ge-or wriggled into the drag sling. Jared would carry their bows and packs. Halfway to their campsite, they would switch positions.

**

The drag had gone more quickly than they had expected, Ge-or staying in the sling the whole way. Revitalizing their fire, the boys cooked and ate their first meal since breaking their fast before first light that day.

As they were cleaning up, Ge-or patted Jared on the shoulder. "A good shot, Brother. Thirty-four paces, down-hill – you set up just right and made the perfect kill. Father will be pleased."

Both of them were happy with the hunt. Their father was a martinet when it came to their weapons training. He hated to see a botched shot, and most especially a wounded animal. He had taught the boys to respect the forest and all that lived in it. When they killed, it was for a purpose. Jared had reviewed every piece of his set-up, movements, aim, and release a dozen times on the way back to their camp. He could find no fault in any part of the hunt. He knew Manfred would have them describe the whole expedition.

Jared sniffed the air. "Snow soon, a nor-wester. Should we move down the slope a league or more, to be closer to the road in case it gets bad?"

Ge-or raised his head from tying one of the deer they had harvested days before to a brace on the sled. He sniffed the air too. "Might get eight inches or more. That'll be rough tomorrow on these narrow trails with the sled, and more-so with the added weight of the cat. Yes, let's get as close to the bottom as we can. The North Coast Road should freeze over tonight and give us ice to glide on for the trek to Permis. Unfortunately, by the time we get far enough down this ridge, the snow will be deep and it will be too late to build any kind of shelter for the night."

Jared gestured to the northwest. "If we head along the old cart path on Bear Ridge, follow that for a league or so, and then cut over on that trapper trail to the north, we could stop just past Old Knobby… make camp in those droopy hemlocks. There are some big ones before that last slope down to the road."

"Let's get started, then. I'll get some good coals in the fire pan; then spread the fire out, while you harness up."

13

Five minutes later Jared was set in the harness. "Ready?" Ge-or almost had to yell. The wind had picked up, presaging the snow and cold to come. He was standing at the back of the sled, downhill side, to help guide it, and push when necessary.

With a last glance around, Jared heaved ahead. By-the-gods, this is heavy, he thought. Thankfully, most of the way this night would be downhill.

Two hours later, Ge-or, in harness again, stopped suddenly. He stood tall, gazing up through the snow swirling in long grey-white rivulet strands about the conifers on the ridge climbing to his left.

Jared, watching carefully, pulled back at the sudden halt. "Again?" he questioned Ge-or.

Ge-or nodded, focusing on the direction the sense of danger was coming from. Something didn't feel right, and it was not the first time on this hunt that his heightened sense of warning had peaked.

"Closer?" Jared asked. The two other times that Ge-or had noticed the uncomfortable pressure behind his eyes, it had seemed further away. Now he was looking only a hundred paces up the ridge from where they had stopped. The darkness and swirling snow, however, precluded even Jared's exceptional eyesight from penetrating the woods more than several score paces from where they stood on the slope.

Glancing back at Jared, Ge-or shrugged. Both lads knew they would never be able to catch whatever was trailing them. All they could do was stay alert, hopefully losing the tracker as the storm intensified even more. Shaking his head in frustration, Ge-or settled back into the harness. He waved at Jared to push, as he heaved forward. It was worrisome – something or someone had taken an interest in their hunt.

Though they had received warnings of bandits in the area, this was different. What he had just sensed was fundamentally malevolent. They would need to be careful.

It was well past midnight when the boys pulled the laden sleigh up next to a large hemlock. Already heavy with snow, the tree would prove a storm-safe place to spend the night. As Ge-or wriggled out of the harness, Jared pushed several branches to the sides, enough for them to crawl under. These large droopy hemlocks often provided northern hunters and trappers with shelter. Jared and Ge-or would be more than comfortable.

It didn't take them long to get settled. Jared prepared a fire area about a foot from the center of the big tree, banking snow against the trunk. Using the coals from the fire tin, he soon had a comforting low-fire going. Reducing to coals, the chunks of hardwood they had carried with them would last long into the night.

They settled into their deerskin ground capes and warm woolen blankets. Soon they were asleep. While the storm raged, the boys had no worries of setting a watch. Any respectable forest creature would be comfortable in its den this night; and though they were concerned about Ge-or's unease earlier, they knew that within an hour their tracks would be completely covered by the heavy snow. As the storm continued to rage, it would be highly unlikely that even an excellent woodsman could find them after that.

Wintry Red

"Hey," Ge-or grumbled.

Jared had just flung an inch of finely powdered snow off his wool cape as he came up from the cocoon he had been wrapped in for the night. Ge-or, half sitting up on his elbows contemplating starting the day, received the cold cloud on his face.

"We need to get moving," Jared said. "I'll dig out the last of the bread and cheese. We should be ready to go by full light. Storm seems to have blown itself out."

Rolling out, Ge-or pushed his way from under the hemlock to their sled. The lads were used to the cold of the north country. What they were more concerned with was that once the sun came out, it would begin to melt last night's dumping. If they didn't make the main road before noon, the going would be tough over the remaining distance with their make-shift sled. Once they reached Permis, they would pick up their sturdy mule for the almost two-day trek back to Thiele. They had left the animal there during their hunt, as the mountain lion would have found a hobbled animal even easier prey than the sheep grazing below where they had been hunting.

Ge-or stood for a couple of minutes scanning the distant ridgeline, while Jared gathered their bedrolls. When he caught his brother's eye, Ge-or shook his head. Whatever or whoever had been following them was no longer within the older lad's range. Hopefully whatever danger had lurked the night before had lost their trail.

"Do you think Mother is better?" Jared asked as Ge-or tightened the last few straps to the sled.

"Worried?"

"Yes," Jared said as tested the strap across his chest. "She seemed to be getting worse before we left. I hope Father took her to the Hag, like he said he would."

"Aye, not sure why he doesn't trust Mother with her. That tea she brewed for us last winter helped with our ague, that's certain. We were both really sick."

16

"Manfred's always been over-protective of Mother – and stubborn, like you, Ge-or," Jared ribbed him.

"Runs in the family, on both sides, Brother," Ge-or pushed back. "Remember that time he told us she set in her heels when she wanted to marry him, even though Father knew it would estrange her from her elven birthright."

"They do love each other. There's no doubt about that. That's why I think he will have finally taken her to the healer. Mayhap, she is better already. If all goes well, we should be there by noon, day after tomorrow, even with our load."

"Ready!" Ge-or said.

"Let's go, then!" Jared shouted, heaving ahead.

Ge-or grunted as he pushed hard on the back brace of the sled.

The boys worked their way through rough country on a diagonal from their sleeping site to the road. Whenever they could use part of an animal trail they made good time, but they were slowed by the many dips and rises this close to the bottom of the ridge they had been following.

Pushing hard, they reached the road west to Permis an hour before noon. Already the sun and spring warmth had melted some of the storm's eight to ten inches of fresh snow. Now the refrozen ice underneath would provide a good surface for the sled to glide on for at least three or four hours. The only difficulties they would face would be the three steady rises that led up to the wilderness town.

***

They were just cresting the second rise, Ge-or in harness pulling, Jared pushing at the back, when raucous shouts ahead alerted them of something wrong. Looking up, they saw a flight of arrows arch up from the spruce on the south side of the road. Seconds later, both lads could see locals aboard mule-drawn wagons being ambushed by bandits, who were now charging from the trees up the slope of the ditch.

Jared, swinging around the sleigh, quickly realized the defenders would not stand much of a chance against the swarming attack. Already several of the villagers had been hit with arrows; the rest were scrambling to find anything they could fight with. As he came to a sprint, passing

17

Ge-or who was shrugging out of the harness, Jared became the weapon that twenty-years of daily training forged him to be.

Pulling back with his three fingers, he felt the tension of the bow... quick lock on target, slide to a stop... release; feeling for another shaft, running again -- nocking, drawing; stop, release, on ahead. Nock, tension, release, run... Tears of anger, gasping for air... close... shoulder bow... sword and long knife work now...

Bandit falling, more robbers scrambling upward – yelling, slashing, stabbing – overwhelming poorly armed and poorly trained villagers; another defender down... another stabbed through, blood gushing from his throat. Two robbers fall, cut by frantic strokes from above. Older boy stabbed, guts spilling out... Protective mother – small blade against long, sharp steel. Two men slashing, beating, driving her down, until all Jared seemed to see was blood.

"Ahhh..."

Jumping at two from the side... Suddenly in the midst... sword and knife flashing in practiced arcs. Heightened awareness – moving with the tide of the fight... Sensing Ge-or on his right. One with his blades, reacting to the flow – parry, thrust, cut, step up, slice across... Blood – gushing. Spin away, slice across, knife block up; dance left, duck, slash back. Blade free, thrust... again, again; punch left – fist and hilt, straight and hard; pull back right, follow-across, slashing, tearing. Down to one knee; set himself... driving with blade, rip back, slam hilt up, catching a thrust, broad slash, spurting warmth across his face. Plant left, stoop under – up again, twist free, following knife through a block, forward lunge, push off with right, stab, high guard, spin... turn... Breathe... Turn... Ge-or?
Breathe... Breathe...

He turned back looking for his brother; seeing him, he said, "It's a bloody mess," and threw up in the snow.

"Jared! You okay? Jared?"

"It's a bloody mess..." Jared repeated, falling to one knee, sobbing. "Father said, 'It's a bloody mess.'"

"I know, Jared – The Qa-ryks, the last fight before he lost his arm... Come. There are those who need our help."

He and Ge-or had known what to do, superbly so, they had been trained by the best; but they had not been prepared for what they HAD to do.

This had not been a well-designed, well-planned, well-executed hunt. It had been an ambush; then, a massacre over-turned on itself.

"Why didn't you tell me!?" Jared's anguish came out as blame.

Ge-or had fought humanoids before – goblins, gzks – the evil ilk of the caves and deep forests. He knew what Jared was trying to grasp. Yet, it had all happened too quickly, without warning. And though they had done what was necessary, what was right, what in warriors' parlance was honorable, it felt of something else.

With his experience Ge-or knew what his brother did not – rarely did one kill another in a void. It always meant something more.

Jared was struggling with "the something more."

They found one woman, badly wounded, with two arrows broken off in her upper back, as well as numerous shallow slices across her chest and thighs – an attempted rape with weapons. They had been able to stop the horror, though the memory would never leave:

Two young girls alive, perhaps six and eight, with shallow defensive stab wounds on their arms when the women had not been able to fully protect them.

A young lad, dead when a tinder box, the only weapon he had in hand, had broken in half.

Two men, one women, and an older lad brutally cut and stabbed trying to defend themselves and the others. These they could not help. They had been at the fore of the fight using what crude weapons they bore. They had only managed to bring down three of the brigands before Jared and Ge-or had launched into the fight.

This had not been done in empty space.

And Ge-or knew that this was not something he could tell his brother in a few words; it had to be explained in a certain way. First, though, he drew his focus to practical things. Therefore, he kept Jared busy. Directing his younger brother as their father would have – keeping him focused on what needed to be done. They bandaged wounds and offered what succor they could. Then they loaded one wagon; the other with a broken wheel would be left, empty. The mother and girls were placed near the front on the softest pelts – the results of a trapping expedition that the bandits planned to plunder. The deceased villagers Jared laid reverently in the back, while Ge-or tossed the dead bandits into the ditch. Finally, they loaded their own gear, skins, and animal carcasses in the wagon, throwing their make-shift sled on top of the thieves. With the other mule trailing, tied to the wagon with a rope, they were ready.

***

Jared, on the wagon seat, heighed the mules ahead. Ge-or, standing to the back right, helped push the laden flatbed to get it started, then moved up to keep an eye on the wounded. He knew they would need to stop as soon as they were far enough away from the site of the ambush for all of them to feel safe. He wanted to check the wounded once again and give Jared a chance to talk. The weight of what they had just done would hit them even harder soon enough.

They pushed steadily for a half league. Then, finding a clean rivulet coming from melting snow off high rocks, Ge-or waved Jared to

20

pull off to the side. After checking that the mother and two girls' bandages were secure and they were resting as comfortably as possible, the lads hobbled and watered the mules.

Grabbing some hard soap, rough cloths, and a thick bristle brush, the brothers stripped, scrubbing while underneath the flow of the icy water melt, working to free their skin, hair, and outer clothing of the gore of the massacre. After drying themselves and dressing in their extra clothes, Jared stood looking into the distance.

Ge-or placed his right hand on his brother's shoulder, getting him to turn his way.

Jared turned slowly, reddening deeply when he looked up. "I am ashamed, Brother."

"It is always thus after a fight."
Jared looked surprised. "You don't show it."
I have fought and killed gzks before," Ge-or said.
Jared nodded.

Ge-or, the elder by three-and-a-half years, had been on farther-ranging trapping expeditions with his father and other villagers than his brother. Several times they had run into aggressive parties of gzks. Ge-or's first encounter with the dangerous forest beasts, cousins to the deep dwelling goblins of the mountains, had been at dusk, as their small band had begun to set up camp.

Ge-or gestured for Jared to climb to the wagon seat. "Come, we will talk as we go."

"Do you remember what I told you of my first time?" Ge-or asked.
"Of the fight?"
"Aye."

The gzks had come in quickly from all sides – Ge-or had drawn his sword, following his father into the fray. It was a short-lived affair.

The forest goblins had no idea they were attacking one of the most renowned weaponsmen in the kingdom. Ge-or had done what his father had trained both his sons relentlessly for – he fought. It had never occurred to him to do otherwise, though he could have tried to hide, waiting for the skirmish with the gzks to resolve.

Ge-or nodded. "Yes, and I told you I felt sick afterward?"

"You didn't throw up," Jared said, hanging his head.

"Nay, brother, I didn't; but they were evil creatures, not our former neighbors, our brother humans. Those brigands in the ditch chose an evil path, but they were still human beings… It is somehow different."

Ge-or had been ashamed after that fight, and he had to admit, a bit nauseous. It was a common reaction for initiates to life and death combat. Yet now he knew it was decidedly different killing fellow humans, no matter that they had turned to evil ways. The only reason he hadn't thrown up this day was that he had focused on Jared, knowing his brother would need his help, as well as his example.

"Father talked with me following that ambush as I am speaking with you now. He told me that fighting, killing, death are dreadful things, brother, whatever creatures one kills. Remember that. There is no glory in it, like we have oft imagined in the quests you and I dream up whilst working in the fields."

"But I am ashamed."

"The shame is from the deed, the taking of life, not because you have done anything wrong. It is good that we have such feelings when we kill. They remind us of who we are and the choices we make. They remind us of the value of life.

"Father said this to me, 'Every death you take will bring shame, for all life is precious.' He was right, Jared. I felt ashamed when I killed those gzks, and I also feel ashamed at what we did this day; though in both cases, what I did was necessary. These robbers were likely honest, hard-working men at one time, full of the dreams of this life. Somehow, they were beaten by it. They lost their honor along the way. It has been a rough winter, and unfortunately the rough north country drives those who can not tame her toward evil ways."

Ge-or paused for a moment, letting Jared think on what he had said. Then... "You remember that early fall day when you were... maybe seven or eight – you and I had gone hunting for squirrels for dinner. Father told me to take you on your first hunt. By then you were already a better archer than me, and you were very excited to go. We always wanted to please Father."

"I remember."

"What happened?"

"I shot a squirrel."

"Very first shot, and it was a tricky one. The squirrel was small and moving fast around a big oak. You led it just right... So, what happened after?"

Jared smiled slightly before answering. "I felt terrible."

"Aye, and you insisted we take the little fellow, bury him, and say prayers over his grave. You would have nothing to do with taking him back and eating him with the others I shot."

"He was so small... I remember I wouldn't shoot another squirrel for several years thereafter."

"Yet you did shoot rabbits, grouse, other creatures, and even a deer before you ever shot another squirrel."

Jared nodded, thinking for a moment. "I... I was so angry..." Jared gestured toward the east. "It was too much at once." A couple of tears leaked from his eyes.

"We did what was right, Jared; but there is yet more to do. We will bring these people back to Permis, and you and I will talk more in the days ahead. I am proud of you, and Father will be too. You fought well, and you took the high road today. Some never find that path.

"You will deal with various emotions over the next days, brother. I will too. It is best if we can talk through them when they become troublesome. Father and Mother will help as well when we get back."

"Ge-or?" When Ge-or looked up, Jared partially turned on the wagon board and pointed to the east.

Ge-or shook his head. "Nay, Jared. Those men we killed were not rooted in evil. What I have been sensing is deeper than their choice to turn to wickedness. It is as Mother described it – a deep sense of something imminently wrong – a 'tweak in the ether, that indicates evil is near,' though I am not sure I understand what she meant by the 'ether'. The sensation is a short, intense pang in the center of my mind that seems to say, 'Pay attention; danger lurks.'"

He paused momentarily, then added, "I have not felt anything since before we last camped. That time it was far more definitive – as if whatever evil out there was specifically interested in me... us. I have rarely had that sensation, and it was always impersonal before – a flash of danger – nothing more."

"We should stay alert then."

"Aye, and I will ask Mother about it when we get back. She said it was a good thing that I have this ability, but not to rely on it – to expect it will always warn me of danger or evil. It is rare amongst the part-elven and not consistent. But it can be invaluable, so I should pay attention when it comes,"

"I feel... I'm not sure how to put it... odd, less than, that I am not able to sense... evil... like you do," Jared said.

"Don't be," Ge-or laughed. "Your eyesight, flexibility, speed, and other elven traits are better than mine. Remember, while Father pushes us to our limits and beyond, he also says, 'to make the most of what we have been given.' Remember, too, that Mother said I may lose the ability as I get older. Who knows, perhaps you will acquire it.

"You are right, though. We should be extra careful, at least until we get home."

Within the hour, they were driving the wagon up to the gates of Permis as the sun settled on the horizon to the west.

***

Darkness was settling on the North Coast, the waning sliver of moon not having appeared yet above the eastern horizon. Mounds of snow showing gray against the black of the tree line slowly seemed to dissolve into the background, as time erased even those features of the landscape. Soon it was only the sound of dripping runoff that suggested there was something other than flat road ahead.

Until…

A shadow deeper than the night emerged from the ditch. Rising like a wraith, the black-robed figure slid as quietly as death itself along the surface, searching, stopping… stooping low; flowing ahead again, bent closer to the roadbed now, stopping when it found things of interest… a broken board, metal pieces, blood – this one could see well enough in the darkness – then once again sinuously ahead.

Halting abruptly at the sound of sharp fangs ripping and tearing flesh from bones, the figure straightened. Other deadly things of the night were busy with corpses below where he stood. "Begone" he hissed. A sudden gesture of a pale-white appendage sent a flurry of sparks in a swath below. The brief flare drove the wild creatures away from their meal, growling in protest.

They would be back.

The flickering light showed him what had happened here. Torn, mutilated bodies of a dozen or more lay in contorted positions about the ditch. The predators had been at them awhile – dismembered bodies and cracked bones were all that was left of some of the marauders; others had yet to be mauled. Licking his thin lips, he turned away. The uncanny deep blackness of his ensorcelled cape wrapped about him again.

Now he knew that his quarry had not been here… just the two he had espied hunting in the hills. Formidable hunters and fighters, the half-breeds had dissected the bandits with sword and knife long before the predators had gotten to them. Aberon, however, was after other game. The two who had done this were of no interest, unless they got in his way. For now, he would set his brethren on their trail; then… he would see.

Aberon looked to the east – his true focus was there. There was power there. A hint of wholeness was twisting the ether in an uncomfortable way. Soon enough, he would deal with that bothersome dung "of the earth;" and then, with that light expunged, the darkness in the North Country would get deeper. He drew his cape closer about his thin frame and slid whence he had come, along the edge of the road. Finally, slipping back into the ditch, he seemed to float effortlessly up the other side into the trees.

It was time to hunt.

Haddock Bend of an Eve

The boys were well rested, having been offered shelter and food, as well as the chance to clean up a bit more. The extended family of the victims of the bandits' attack had taken them in for the night. Thankfully, the Permis Hag was well versed in the treatment of wounds. The injured would survive.

Considering the tough times, Ge-or and Jared gave the family one of their deer carcasses, the braces of rabbits and squirrels they had hunted, and all the wolf pelts they had harvested during the hunt for the lion. They also gave them the small amount of coinage, weapons, tools, and other miscellaneous items they had garnered from the bandits' packs and bodies after the fight. It was a small haul – the robbers had indeed been desperate after the hard winter. Combined with the pelts from the trapping expedition, the villagers should do well enough for a couple of seasons. Ge-or and Jared figured Manfred would not mind the gifting of the wolf pelts and the food animals. The cougar's meat, however, they gave to the village mayor to distribute to others in need.

That left Ge-or and Jared with only one deer, the caped-out lion's hide, and the five silver for killing the mountain lion. However, as a gesture of thanks, the town's mayor gifted them with a fat milk goat from his own stock. Now they would be able to make even better time, as Nelly would not be so overloaded, nor would they have heavy packs to carry. The boys left Permis just as the sun was peeking over the eastern horizon.

Though the goat slowed them a bit, Nelly wasn't exactly an archetype of forward motion herself. The boys trotted ahead, each with a long halter to gently encourage the animals to move along. They were used to several hours of weapons practice before the sun rose, followed by sparring sessions, work in the fields, and more. Walking and occasionally jogging with the animals most of the day would be tiring, but not wearing.

They planned to cut off the North Coast Road about two-thirds of the way home. Haddock Bend was a community of several houses and cabins, a lodge/tavern, blacksmithy, and small general store set at the crossroads with a trapping trail. It was about a thousand paces or so south of the main road. There they could rest in a room to themselves with a chance to take a long hot bath – their first after almost ten days in the wild. Then they would enjoy the lodge's hearty winter stew the tavern was known for, mugs of hoppy ale, and finally, a soft bed. This would set them up for an early start the next morning. Their plan was to reach Thiele by mid-day. It was after dusk when they reached the outpost.

Things were going well up until their second mug of the strong ale.

Ge-or and Jared had selected a small table near the center of the wall on the left side of the tavern as one entered. Manfred had taught them to always find a spot where they could observe the entire establishment and, most importantly, where they could watch the exits.

Feeling relaxed after their hot baths and their meal of lamb stew, they had decided to splurge on another ale. Suddenly, Ge-or sat upright, signaling Jared. Pivoting on the bench, he swung toward the entrance. A second later the main double doors to the barroom slammed into the heavy log walls. A monster of a man clad all in black strode through the doors, stopped two paces in, and scanned the room. The fellow had to weigh in at more than fifteen stone and was heavily muscled, dirty, and unshaven. He carried more than a few wicked-looking, though unusual, weapons about his person – an odd two-bladed sword anchored somehow in a back scabbard with the blades sticking up; three wavy snake knives of various lengths stuck in his thick belt; a mace – its flanges sharpened, rather than the usual heavy blunt ones, also in his belt; and a nasty spiked club in his left fist. The man's hardened leather armor was a deep black, making him look like more than a bit of trouble.

Strange and frightening as this man appeared, what set the two boys on edge was a small, cowled man, dressed also completely in black, who stepped in at the side of the behemoth fighter. This gnarled, shrunken, monk-like figure seemed to radiate evil; or so the two boys, and obviously many of the patrons, felt, for chairs were pushed back and hands moved toward belt knives. All one could see of the monk or priest was his two hands, which were white-pale extending from the voluminous sleeves of his heavy robe. He moved in with an odd shuffling gait that made him appear even more sinister.

As the small man noisily scuffled ahead toward the bar, Ge-or sensed that this being had been the source of the forewarnings he had noted several times during their hunt. This close, he seemed to sense a noisome odor waft through the room – something intangible that not only felt of evil, but embodied it through scent and feel. The rest of the customers seemed to echo what he was feeling, pushing back from the man as far they could.

Melrose, the owner and barkeep of Haddock Bend, also a formidably-sized man, tried to smile when the monk in black stepped up to the bar. It was all he could do to keep from shrinking back, though the small man's partner had made no move to come closer.

"Rooms," the dark monk squealed in a high-pitched, grating voice, making what normally would have been a question into a demand with a threat attached.

Before Melrose could answer, the small man shrilled, "And clear these people out of here," gesturing about the room.

Ge-or and Jared, who had both risen at the threat, stayed where they were, yet many patrons began to comply. Though this pair looked formidable, he and Jared were confident in their abilities to defend themselves. The big man's array of weapons were impressive; however, they both knew that most of them were for show. They would be unwieldy even in accomplished hands.

Sidling toward the tavern's weapons rack, the two boys appeared to be following the priest's directive. Melrose had set one on each side of the room for any weapons larger than a long knife – customers' extra blades, bows, and other weapons were expected to be placed on the racks when they came in. Ge-or and Jared had specifically chosen their table to be within several paces of where they had placed their weapons.

Looking down and away, so as not to raise suspicion, Ge-or picked up his sword while his back was to the room. And a second after tying his quiver to his thigh, Jared had his bow with an arrow nocked in his left hand.

"Clear out!" The behemoth growled, gesturing in the direction of Ge-or and Jared, who had turned and were now facing the door, standing stolidly next to the weapons rack.

"Set One," Ge-or said loudly, shifting into ready position for weapons form number one. He hoped the fellow knew what the basic forms were for bladed weapons, because the man would at least understand that Ge-or was not a boy who was playing at being brave.

Jared set himself into the holding position for archery line practice, his fingers lightly gripping the arrow in place on the nock, waiting. Both were now fully facing the two men.

The monk or priest made some sort of motion with his left hand; and since both boys had no experience with those who could use power, they half expected something to shoot out at them from the man's pale appendage. Instead, the big man raised the club in his left hand and took two steps toward them, brandishing it menacingly.

"Two," Ge-or shouted, snapping into fighting position one, with his sword balanced on his left arm, tip of the blade pointed at his opponent. Jared drew back, his arrow now aimed at the monster's throat knot; though there was no like command in archery, he was playing along with Ge-or's show of confidence.

Movement in the room had now stopped. Those patrons who hadn't made it outside were standing frozen in place. Melrose was standing behind the bar, not knowing what to do. Normally his presence was enough to get troublemakers to at least pause if he spoke. Right now, aside from having brought the club he always kept handy up high enough that it could be seen by everyone, he had no idea how to respond to these two characters. The one looked like he could actually rip his arms from their sockets; the other, as if he might cause a bolt of lightning to come down that would blast him to the Nine Planes of Hell. Plus, the two young lads, sons of Manfred of Borea, the great fighter of the first Qa-ryk Wars, were standing up to, and obviously ready to take on, these two.

It was another voice that broke through the tension. "Hold! Hold this foolishness."

No one, except Melrose, Ge-or, and Jared, had seen the door open. At the word "foolishness," another powerfully built person, dressed in a brown, cowled, heavy wool robe, strode into the tavern. He scanned the room and yelled again. "Enough, Arpol, or you and I will have it out right here, instead of in a more appropriate venue outdoors."

The black priest turned toward the figure now framing the doorway. The small man then appeared to cringe, taking a step backward while dropping his hands to his side.

At that motion, Jared released most of the tension of his draw, bringing the bow halfway down from eye level. Ge-or slowly eased out of his fighting stance.

"Go back to your foul brethren, Arpol. These people don't scare as readily as the farmers and ranchers in your usual haunts. Else you and Brack will find yourself skewered sooner than you would like. Begone. Your stink is fouling the place, and I thought to stay here myself this night."

"You trust your powers too much, worm of the Earth," the black priest hissed. "We go where we will and do what we desire. But now that you are here, we would get no rest with the stench of Gaia in the air." Arpol pointed toward the door with his chin. He and Brack began to move slowly toward the exit, as the newcomer strode confidently further into the room.

Jared was about to lower his bow further, when he saw movement on Brack's right side. A throwing knife had appeared; and the huge man's hand came back quickly, readying it to throw at the brown-clad priest.

Jared's bow came up more quickly, and he was at full draw by the time it reached eye level. He released immediately. The shaft flew true, piercing Brack's wrist in the center. The brute howled, dropping his knife. The arrow sliced completely through the wrist, sticking low in the door behind.

Arpol spun around looking at Brack, who had dropped his club and was cradling his injured hand. Then he spun toward Jared, who was already nocking another arrow. Ge-or had moved at Jared's shot and was partway to the door, his sword raised. The dark priest turned quickly back; grabbing Brack's arm, he pulled him through the portal. The doors swung shut, leaving the Earth cleric looking toward Jared and Ge-or.

"I am an initiate of the Earth. I thank you for your help." The brown clad priest bowed toward the two brothers. This man of the cloth was young. He looked sturdily built, though his voluminous robes hid much of his body; and he moved easily, like a man who had trained physically. With his cowl now lowered, the boys could see that the man's head was completely shaven except for a thin line above his forehead. He brushed at the tuft of hair and grinned. "I am afraid that until my hair grows back completely, I can give you no name. We do not receive our ministerial appellation until our initiate period is complete. If you wish to address me, please use 'Earth Father,' 'Earth Cleric,' or the like. I am at your service. Neither of you are injured?"

Ge-or, after looking over at Jared, shook his head. "Thank you, good Earth Father; neither of us was hurt. I am Ge-or of Thiele, my brother, Jared." The two boys bowed. Then Ge-or asked, "Are those two dangerous?"

"Not as much as they would like you to think. Arpol is a follower of the Black Druids, likely an acolyte of their dark ways. He has power; but it is limited, I sense. He has learned that bluster and an overly large companion who looks dangerous open many doors. Truthfully, I do not think he knew I was back on his trail."

While Earth Father answered, Jared noticed that the cleric was patting his voluminous robe, as if searching for something. Then, as Ge-or began to ask another question, the priest's hand slipped into a small pocket.

"You have been following them?"

Withdrawing a small object, the Earth Cleric immediately began to toy with it – moving the rondelle about in his hands in what looked to be a practiced motion; rubbing it with his fingers.

As Father Earth answered Ge-or's query, Jared seemed fascinated by what appeared to be the intricately carved, circular piece of hardwood.

"One of my initiate tasks is to connect with the villages along the North Coast, helping where I can. Accomplishing that, I am to travel

32

south and west into more dangerous lands to learn more about these black priests. I have been following that…, well, shall I say… dark piece of a hind's butt for several weeks…" Earth Father smiled. "Since I ran into them near Cutter-by-the-Sea, we have been playing the child's game of 'touch and go'.

"Pardon me, I jabber a bit… One of my penances, coming from my training, is to learn the blessing of silence. I tend to like the sound of my own voice, hah!"

"Are you a healer, Father?" Jared asked, thinking of their mother.

"You have need of me?"

"You may be of help to us, if you are willing to come to Thiele in the morning. We plan to leave early though, at dawn or before."

"Thiele, ah, yes, last village along the coast. That is indeed fortuitous, then; for I am actually headed that way. And though I am only an initiate to the Path of Gaia, I have always had a propensity for helping those with their physical ailments. My strength comes from the earth… How may I serve?"

"Our mother took ill this past fall," Jared answered. "She has been struggling with a fever and chills all winter. We are returning home from a hunting expedition. While our hopes are that her symptoms have abated, if you have healing skills, we would appreciate your looking in on her. We have money and can pay."

"No need for that, we Earth Brothers serve as we may. We ask only for sustenance and a place to stay, if such is available. I will do what I can for your mother, as well as provide assistance to your village. As you may imagine, I have been busy this difficult winter. I will likely need to stay for several days to help all those I may."

Father Earth paused, making sure he caught both the boys' eyes. It was then that he noticed their high cheekbones, the slight elongation of their ears upward, and other racial features. Jared, especially, seemed to have a slim, lithe body-type, though he was still young enough that he had yet to fill out completely. It was hard to be sure, because the elven matured later than humans; but these two appeared to be young adolescents. He blinked. "You are part elven?"

Jared and Ge-or both nodded, speaking at the same time, "Our mother is elven…" Jared smiled. Stopping, he let Ge-or continue.

"Does it matter for a healing?"

"No, though different racial backgrounds can affect what disharmonies of the body may afflict a person. I am willing to come with you and help if I can. I will need to speak with her as well as examine her with my energy. It is important that you understand, though, that healers have limitations.

"Do you have a local Hag?"

Jared and Ge-or both nodded.

"That is good. Has she been treating your mother?"

"We're not sure," Ge-or said. "Father was reluctant to take her. He is stubborn and does not trust local herbalists altogether. We tried to convince him to take Mother to her."

"Will he abide a cleric?"

Ge-or answered, "I think he might – a cleric saved his life when he lost his arm during the Qa-ryk Wars."

"Good. I will meditate on it this night; then I will see your mother on the morrow."

"What is that in your hand, Earth Father?" Jared asked, his curiosity returning to the medallion the Earth Cleric was still toying with.

"Ah, this." He held up the object so they could see it better. "I forget sometimes that I toy with it. It is a device of my religion, given me for my initiate. I will receive a more powerful symbol once I pass through my trials and become a full-fledged cleric. Such tokens help us to focus our inner energy; often they are imbued with power as a protection against evil.

"My mentor, Sart, a newly anointed priest, made it for me, to celebrate my initiation. Here." He held the piece out even further. "See. The circle or wreath represents Mother Gaia; the roots crossing the center, our connection to the earth; and the cross represents my penchant for healing."

"It helps you heal?" Jared asked.

"In a way, yes. The wood is quite dense – black walnut, which can store earth energy better than many other types; and, if you look closely, note the small garnet in the center, where the roots meet. Gems also store energy, and garnets help with healing better than many other gems."

Jared could see the trundle was quite worn from rubbing. He reached out for it, but Earth Father quickly withdrew his hand.

"Sorry, my son, but I keep it with me always. Only rarely do I let others touch it, and that is when I do a healing. I place it on a person's forehead or sometimes elsewhere on the body, where their disease is centered."

"My mistake, Father." He lowered his head.

"You knew not… Come, I am in need of sustenance, and we can talk more over food and drink. Can I buy you an ale? Food?"

"We have eaten, but will be happy to finish our mugs with you," Jared said. "Please sit, Father of the Earth. I will see to your meal. They have a hearty winter stew here and solid bread to dip in it."

"A true blessing, then. Now that we are free of that vile creature and his massive companion, I will enjoy a fulfilling meal."

"I'll get your arrow, Jared," Ge-or said, "while you get the good cleric some food. We should be to bed soon, though. It's been a long day."

Boys will be Boys – or Not

Though it took Melrose's deep bass voice and the ringing of the tavern's loud dinner bell to entice many of the patrons back, the large tavern room was soon almost full of those who were curious about "What had happened?" Soon the place had three times the clientele than before the incident.

By the time Melrose got a short break to come over to their table, Earth Father had finished his meal; and the boys were ready to head up to their room.

"Please, young Jared, a half hour or so. I'll cover all your expenses and pay a silver to boot. What say ye?"

Ge-or shrugged; he had no talent for music at all. This was all on his brother's shoulders. Jared finally nodded tiredly. He loved to sing; plus, saving the money for their stay would please their father. "One hour only, Mel," Jared said, knowing that the innkeeper would keep him playing half the night in spite of what he had said. "We're beat, and we need to get off in the morning."

Melrose nodded his head vigorously. Manfred brought Lililia with both boys there for dinner once or twice a month when he came to trade. Jared's high tenor blended well with the deep baritone of Sendar – a travelling lutenist who worked the North Coast taverns for tips, ale, food, and a place to stay. When they visited, Jared would join the troubadour for a couple of hours of singing the local drinking and dancing songs. Mel would cover Manfred's bill on these occasions. If people knew the family would be coming, Mel's tables would be full. Sendar had just come in; and Mel was hoping that with Jared's addition, the people who had come for news would stay longer to hear his beautiful voice and hence spend more money on drink.

Melrose had just left their table, when he thought of something else. He turned back, motioning for Jared to follow him. When they got to the bar, Mel went behind and fished around, moving barrels and other items to get what he had stored far in the corner. He pulled out a well-worn portable harp.

"A travelling jongleur had it with him. I used to let him perform for food and drink, like Sendar does now – 'twas an old fellow. He passed in his sleep one night. I've kept it, thinking someone might come for it; but that was a while back now. Since then, I forgot I had it. I remember Lililia said she was looking for an instrument – lyre, small harp – for you to learn on. Do you think this might do?"

Jared was astounded. He had yearned for an instrument of some sort, since his mother had promised to teach him to play. He could see it needed to be repaired in places, cleaned, polished, and restrung. It was rosewood, the sounding board spruce – the combination of woods would be beautiful and have a strong resonance when reglued and patched.

"How much?" he stammered. He knew that Melrose would not part with it cheaply, though he had got it for nothing himself.

"Eight silver, and that's a bargain. They sell for thrice that or more east of the King's Wall."

"Four, you old miser. The thing is in dreadful shape – else I won't sing for you anymore." Jared and Ge-or had both been privy to their father's haggling in the fur market. Though he desperately wanted the instrument, he was trying not to show how much.

"Seven and not a copper less, I've had to store…"

"Take five," Earth Father said, having come up behind Jared. "Once the boy learns to play it, you will have the better of the bargain." He slapped a gold piece on the bar top.

"I cannot take your coin, good Father," Jared said.

"I will hear you sing. If you do not please, you can pay me back when we reach Thiele. Once you fix it, you will provide pleasure to those who travel about this world like myself, and that will be my reward as well. Many times, the only music I hear during my wanderings is the wolves howling of a night, accompanied by crickets, coyotes, and screech owls." Earth Father pushed the gold piece toward Melrose. "Give the boy the portative and me my change."

The innkeeper grudgingly accepted Earth Father's terms.

Jared sang, and occasionally accompanied Sendar with an alto recorder from a set that Melrose kept. Earth Father was more than pleased with Jared's performance. There were times when Sendar's luxurious baritone, blending with Jared's light tenor, had him and many other patrons sniffling into a handy cloth.

It was midnight by the time Jared managed to get away to bed. Ge-or and Earth Father had gone up over an hour earlier.

In spite of the late night, Ge-or and Jared were up before dawn as they had pledged; but they did not beat Earth Father. They found him meditating when they came out. His feet were bare, as he stood next to a snow and ice pile near the tavern door. As they came up, he stretched his arms toward the eastern horizon.

"Well met, my young hunters – a beautiful morning for our trip west. Thank the gods for that. I had Melrose's wife make us roasted lamb and bread concoctions with grilled onions and new oregano. I am drooling already, though I will stay my hand for a while. We thank the Earth Mother for her bounty and her challenges, too.

"I might add," he said with a twinkle in his eyes, "that I managed to talk my way into a short keg of ale from Mel for our jaunt to Thiele, he was so pleased with your singing. Gaia and her blessings to us." He began to whistle a lively tune, which had the effect of bringing a scruffy-looking donkey from around the side of the building. It came up to the Earth Cleric, nudging him forcefully in the side.

"Oof," the Earth Father said. "All right, I have it. One moment, you mangy creature. Ah, here it is." He pulled a carrot from one of what must have been more than a few pockets lining the inside of the brown robes he wore.

"Here, meet two young men from our next destination. Ge-or the Bold and Jared of the Bow and Sweet Voice." He bowed with a flourish toward the two brothers.

Jared groaned under his breath. Considering their efforts the past week and little sleep, an overly boisterous companion might make his vague headache even worse.

The Earth Father must have noticed Jared's discomfort. "Come here, lad, I have just the thing for that fog overhanging your disposition this morn. Drink this." He handed over a small vial of clear liquid, also taken from somewhere about his robe.

Jared shook the small bottle, then looked at Ge-or, who shrugged. Jared shrugged too, sniffed at the bottle, then downed the potion in one long swallow. It tasted a good bit like peppermint combined with other herbs. It seemed to cool his throat as it went down, then his stomach, and finally, he would have sworn, he could feel it coursing through his veins. By the time he handed the vial back, he was feeling amazingly well.

***

Earth Father proved an animated trail companion. If he was indeed on a penance of silence, he was hardly ever making amends, because he was almost constantly chatting to the brothers; or, if they were busy with the animals, having an oddly-balanced conversation with his mule, who he referred to as "Dumpy."

As they made their way along the western path from Haddock Bend back to the North Coast Road, Earth Father plied both boys with questions. Trained to see ill-ease of many sorts, he used the time to draw them out. Jared especially seemed to be struggling with something. By the time they were approaching the rise leading up to the road, the boys had opened up considerably about what they had been through. And as they encouraged the two mules and the goat up the steep rocky path, both Ge-or and Jared seemed to be much more relaxed. Their banter about which animal would win the odd "race" to the top had even Earth Father laughing. It seemed the right time to change the direction of their conversation.

Earth Father had begun to understand that these lads, being part-elven, were in many ways still boys, not adults. He knew that human development mimicked part-elven and elven maturation until about year five. After those early years, however, the growth process for elves and the part-elven changed, slowing dramatically. Human boys of twelve or thirteen were starting to reach basic sexual maturity. A half-elven lad wouldn't reach that maturation point until he neared twenty-five? More? He actually didn't know – and the elven, many years past that. Thus, though Jared and Ge-or looked to be ten to fourteen years of age, they were likely much older.

This spiked his interest, because what he had seen of the lads, from Jared's fine shot to Ge-or's confidence, spoke to a tale that their youthful appearance belied.

Once they had settled onto the Permis-Thiele Road, Earth Father decided to ask them about their training. "That was a remarkable shot you made in the tavern, Jared. While Brack is more show than bite, you may have saved me or someone else from being injured."

Jared looked puzzled, so Ge-or answered. "That shot? Jared could have made it at thrice the distance. He's the best archer on the North Coast, won the crown the past two years running."

"And Ge-or has won the sword crown the last three!"

"The crown? Truly?" Earth Father was amazed. Weaponry contests were fairly common throughout Borea. They encouraged those in dangerous environs to maintain a degree of fighting ability. However, it was quite extraordinary that two young lads, half eleven or not, would take the highest regional award for the open level – professionals and general populace.

"You have had training, then?"

"With our father, Manfred of Borea," Ge-or answered proudly.

"I know not that name."

Both Ge-or and Jared looked strangely at Earth Father. "THE Manfred of Borea, the most renowned swordsman of the Qa-ryk Wars," Jared said.

"Sorry. Though I ply a mace now and again, I know little else about weaponry. I'm afraid I have spent much of my life in studious pursuits, having been brought up at a monastery. We Earth Birds – sorry, Clerics of Gaia – are a wandering lot. Our primary mission is to help others through our healing ministry, though my mentor has encouraged me to learn to protect myself.

"Would you lads be willing to show me some of your skills?"

Ge-or looked at Jared. "Too early for dove; and though there are pigeons about, they are not a favorite for dinner. What of turkey, Jared? I saw a few in the trees yesterday. I might be able to chase some out of the spruce alongside the road this early in the day." He looked toward the low ridge that rose from the ditch alongside the road bed.

"You're right, Ge-or, they should already be settling in to roost – roust them out."

Ge-or started for the ditch, talking as he went. "Watch closely, Earth Father, he's fast. I've seen him wing doves in season."

"Winging a dove?" Earth Father asked.

Jared answered as Ge-or edged down the side of the road until he was working his way amongst the spruce that dotted the hillside. "We set up between a feed lot, like a corn field or sunflower field, and a water source, such as a pond or stream, near dusk. Doves will fly from the fields to the water before settling down for the night. We shoot them 'on the wing,' in other words, out of the air."

"A dove?"

"Sure. Once you get used to them, they fly fairly straight. You only have to gauge their speed and direction."

"But they're quite small."

"True. Ge-or and I rarely hunt them unless there are plenty, which is only in the late summer and early fall. Takes about fifteen or so for a family meal. You only eat the breasts – we make a stock of the rest."

Ge-or knew that during the spring the turkeys liked to scrounge where the brush was thick and the trees offered a roost, so he worked that area close to the road. After about fifteen minutes, he yelled up to Jared who was walking on the road parallel to his brother. "Gobbler, Jared! He's running ahead of me… Staying down… He's up! Still low…" Ge-or kept Jared apprised of the bird's movements.

Two minutes later, Ge-or waved from below. "He didn't want to come out. Settled back. I'll chase him up again. The hens are running ahead... Wait! There he is; just ahead… Breaking left and… he's up! Sailing south. You have a shot?"

Jared reacted at, "he's up." Pulling his bow from his shoulder in one smooth motion, he already had an arrow in his other hand from his

41

thigh quiver. At "You have…," his bow was ready with arrow nocked; and Jared had it at full draw, when Ge-or reached "a shot?" The turkey was now twenty-five paces out and moving fast. Before Earth Father realized it, Jared had released. He saw the shaft sailing on an arc up over the ditch toward the spruce. The shaft hit dead center as the turkey began to descend. The big bird tumbled into the heavy brush.

"By-the-gods of the Earth, Sun, and Moon!" Earth Father exclaimed. "I have never seen shooting like that. More than thirty paces out, moving away, and 'on the wing,' as you said."

Ge-or raced ahead, quickly retrieving the turkey and Jared's arrow. "Dinner tonight," he said, grinning, as he climbed back up to the road. "Good shot, brother. Mother will be pleased."

"Truly amazing!" Father Earth said.

"Practice," Ge-or stated. "Father drives us daily from dawn to dusk, and oft before and after."

"Ge-or likes to brag about my bow skills, but he is the best swordsman I have ever seen. He beats our father in an even spar now. He is also the best I have seen at the standard forms. Perfection itself."

"Forms?" Earth Father questioned.

Ge-or answered, "Practice sets designed for a variety of weapons. They help to teach discipline, offensive and defensive moves, develop strength and flexibility, and so on. Each form is designed to succeed against certain types of weapons and attacks. Dozens of forms have been developed for a wide variety of weapon types."

"And you know them all?"

Ge-or nodded. "We have practiced them for hours a day for years. We now use them to stay in shape and to serve as jumping off places for creative weapons play. Would you like to see us spar using Form One for the short sword?"

"We could take a bit of a break," Earth Father offered. "For one, I could use a quaff from that barrel."

Ten minutes later, refreshed from a short rest and half a mug of ale, the two lads faced each other in the middle of the road.

It took less than two minutes. After their formal introductory moves, Father Earth saw only the flash of blades their movements were so fast. What was obvious was that for every strike one made, the other had a block. It was almost a dance of sorts. They were amazingly efficient and accurate in what they did, else they would have shaved off some part of the other's anatomy.

Earth Father bowed to each in turn when they finished. "Impressive. It is something to see – a thing of beauty, but also of death. I am amazed at your skills, yet I imagine you take your father's training far beyond these 'forms.'"

"They serve mostly as a foundation," Ge-or offered. "A person only uses the forms against men and weapons, or creatures and weapons, that are not familiar with them. Using the forms against another expert is, in many ways, an exercise in futility. The winner is the one who makes a mistake first, or who simply dies of exhaustion," he grinned.

"Or," Jared pushed his brother in the shoulder playfully, "one steps out of the forms and creates something that your opponent cannot defend against. Creative use of weaponry is the next level in learning to be a master weaponsman."

"I guess I can understand that. Unfortunately, though I have been trained recently in the use of the mace, I am a bit of a 'masher,' I believe they say. I wade into a fight and do my best. I could probably learn a great deal from both of you. Have you wielded maces in your training?"

"Of course, Ge-or answered. "We practice all forms of common weaponry, as well as oddities our father has accumulated over the years."

"Why?"

"I'm not sure," Ge-or said. "I guess he has seen so much fighting and death, that he wants us to be prepared for anything. It is a difficult life here in the north... Bandits and thieves, and... well, rumors of Qa-ryks expanding their range again..."

"Gzks, goblins and the like," Jared added.

"Dark priests, like..."

"Arpol," Earth Father answered. "Come, let us on our way. We will talk more as we walk. I wouldst examine your mother before dark."

Encouraging the animals with rope halters, the three walked closely together. Ge-or almost immediately asked. "Who or what were those two at Haddock's Bend? Even Melrose was afraid of them."

"Arpol and Brack?" Earth Father said. "Followers of the Black Druids – priests who twist nature to their own evil ways. It is why I have followed those two occasionally during my ministries along the North Coast – to learn more of their purposes. Brack is mostly for show; a brute, nothing more. Arpol, more dangerous. As a priest he…"

"Agggh…" Suddenly Ge-or grabbed his forehead with his right hand and groaned, falling to one knee in the slush of the road.

"Ge-or," Jared shouted, heading toward his brother.

Earth Father waved him back; grabbing his rondelle as he stepped up to Ge-or. Kneeling, he pushed Ge-or's hand aside and pressed the circular medallion to the boy's forehead. Closing his eyes, he began to chant in High Elvish. Jared only caught a few words. "Peace… the world will grant… of the earth… So be it."

Standing, Earth Father helped Ge-or to his feet. "Better, my son?"

Ge-or nodded. Took a few deep breaths, then looked at Jared.

"The premonition?"

Ge-or nodded again. "Really strong this time." He pointed to the south. "Help me up. I…"

Jared immediately stood, pulling Ge-or up with him. They both began scanning the ridge to the south, Ge-or holding his brother's shoulder to steady himself.

"****

Aberon felt the cold tip of an ice dagger slowly make its way up his backbone, opening a blood red gash all along his spine, a cut that did not bleed, but was felt intensely. The cold blade twisted inward when it reached the hollow just above the base of his head; the agony forced him to one knee. It was an anguish relived – delivered by one such as he was now. He shivered uncontrollably for several seconds, while desperately spinning a web of hiding with his left hand. But that was not the worst… slowly, inch by inch, he felt the gash knit back together – intense tingling and itching with the pain – another sensation that told him he would soon

44

be free of the memory, but not yet. At the end, terror, as the ice turned to fire with the torturous, turning removal of the blade... He fell to his side.

He woke, shivering from his own sweat. Laying there upon the still icy ground, he knew that had been close. The one boy had been sensitive to Aberon's aura. He would need to be more careful.

Aberon stood now, still protected by the shielding web. He looked down to the road as the three wayfarers continued on their way. Thankfully he had seen the Earth Cleric rise and had had time to hide himself in spite of the pain from the terrible memory his use of so much energy had elicited.

No matter. They were headed for the last village along the Coast Road. He could step back and wait to see what happened. That fool Arpol had gone too close, and Brack had been wounded. Now, even with healing bindings, the brute would be useless for three days... Almost useless – he would set them to follow these three. With orders to make no contact.

His time would come. He doubted the two half-elven would join the priest once he left that village for the south. For now, Aberon, Black Priest, minion of the dark Druids, would gather energy. He would prepare himself to face the only one that mattered.

***

"Premonition?" Earth Father asked.

"He sometimes senses evil," Jared answered. "Ge-or inherited it from our mother. Someone, something, has been following us the past two days."

"I thought it might be Arpol," Ge-or said. "I felt it again when he came into the tavern. Just now, it was very strong. I felt dizzy, sick almost, and a strong flash of pain in my forehead. Coming from the south. Though I don't sense it now."

"How much warning do you typically have?"

"Hard to say," Ge-or answered. "I feel this pressure in my head – I can sense where it comes from, but I have never seen anything. You think those two are following us?" Ge-or asked.

"More likely me, and you have just been in the way. It is possible they sent a searching conjuration, and that is what affected you so strongly. Let me know if you sense anything again. Perhaps it is time I discouraged those two."

***

They were now about an hour and a half east of Thiele. Earth Father had kept an eye on Ge-or, but the two boys had soon relaxed and were enjoying boyish banter. It reminded Earth Father of his interest in their heritage.

"May I ask something of you both? I have rarely met the half-elven or part-elven, and find the age and maturation similarities and differences to that of humans an interesting consideration."

"What do you wish to know, Father?" Jared asked.

"It would seem to me that it would be difficult for you to see the friends you played with as youngsters grow so much faster than you. Most, I would assume, must be married and settled by now?"

Jared shrugged. "Aye, we," he gestured toward Ge-or, "see them about the village; and though we still acknowledge what we used to do together, it feels like that fades more and more each year. And younger lads we could be friends with quickly realize that our approach to life is different. Truth is, we ARE different because of what we have been through and what we have learned."

"One major difference is that we both read and write the common tongue, as well as High Elvish. Few people in our village read and write at all. It is, in a way, embarrassing for them, and for us, to be asked to read some document for our former playmates. I think it is one reason Father, and Mother too, have kept us learning so many different things. He tries to keep us busy, because we don't have other youngsters our age and training to… well, have fun with anymore, to do things with.

"We are, in a sense, caught between our youth and adulthood. Luckily, we have each other, which serves to some extent to mitigate those differences with others."

"What other things do your parents encourage you to learn?" Father Earth asked.

46

Ge-or smiled. "They both push us to learn everything we can."

"Ge-or has formed his own sword," Jared jumped in. "He has been working with the smith for several years, and I am to start this fall."

"The work has improved my strength, and more than that – I have learned the workings of metal, the makings of weapons, much more."

"We have made our own bows, arrows, and other equipment, too," Jared added.

"All of these help us to better ourselves in general, like learning discipline, control, focus; as well as, I suppose, keep us busy," Ge-or laughed.

Earth Father was beginning to understand how much different they were from typical human lads just approaching adulthood. There was a confidence, enthusiasm, and a certain bearing that spoke of what Ge-or had just mentioned – discipline, control, and much more – they had a certain poise and character that was much older than the age they looked to be.

"We have learned many other things, too." Jared began to list them – "Forestry, farm work, boating and fishing, and...

"Mother has taught us household duties as well," Ge-or interrupted, "though I have never taken much to cooking."

Jared nodded vigorously to that admission.

"And often," Ge-or added, "we have learned through apprenticing to local craftsman – like the smith, tanner, woodworker, bowyer and fletcher, and so on."

"We have..."

"Hold, hold," Earth Father grinned. He was about to ask another question when he saw the boys' shoulders suddenly droop, as they began to understand how different they were. The reality was beginning to weigh on their thoughts. Instead he said, "Come, let us stop for our mid-day meal and then press on to Thiele. I look forward to meeting your parents."

After they had eaten, Earth Father figured it was not his place to push the boys further. He had woken them a bit more to their situation, and they were both bright enough to ponder for themselves what direction their lives might take. For one thing, the younger boy had a true talent for music, and that might be just the thread to build a life upon. The older? He would find a niche, perhaps as his father had. Both boys were bright and able.

There was one thing that was concerning him, and it came to the surface as they were sitting and eating their meal – what interest did Arpol have in these young lads? He WAS dangerous. Earth Father would need to watch carefully to see if those two evil maggots were following Ge-or and Jared, or whether that was just chance because of his own interest in their wanderings about the north country.

He would follow them again once he had finished his work at Thiele. It was time he began the more serious aspect of his own work – finding out more about these Dark Priests.

The Edge of the West

They could see the gates of Thiele ahead, open and inviting, a few villagers just inside. The boys glanced over their shoulder. Earth Father waved them ahead. They had given him directions to their cabin. To give the lads time to be with their parents, he would follow a bit more slowly.

Jared and Ge-or were welcomed by everyone they saw on the way to their house. Many admired the mountain lion pelt. Since the mountain lion had been marauding all winter in a neighboring town's pastures, the outcome was of particular importance. Once a cat this large had established itself, it was likely more would follow. Now that was far less likely.

As they neared their house, they knew something was not quite right. Though their immediate neighbors were friendly and acknowledged them, they tended to look away or down; and they did not engage in the banter other people had. Ge-or and Jared picked up their pace and were jogging as they came around the last corner.

Their father met them at the door. Manfred grasped each of their wrists, acknowledging their return; yet, he also averted his eyes. For a moment, both Ge-or and Jared thought their mother might have passed this very day; but a moment later a soft voice from within said, "Come, boys, I would see you this bright day. Have you had success?"

They ran in through the main cabin room into the bedroom. Their mother was sitting in a rocking chair their father had made a couple of years before. When she had become ill the past fall, she had spent more and more time in it, able to sit in the sun and look out the one window that their father had set there for that purpose. When they saw her, they knew why their father was so despondent. Lililia was wan, with a yellowish tinge to her skin. It seemed an effort even to move her hands up to greet each of them with a hug.

Both of the boys had tears in their eyes when they stepped back. "Mother, Mother," Jared said, "we have brought a priest with us from Haddock Bend. He is 'of the Earth' and said he would help you."

As a healer, Earth Father was warmly welcomed with nods, bows, and handshakes as he wended his way through the houses. Followers of Gaia were always welcome because of the healings and blessings they freely offered. He took time to acknowledge all who came up to him. He knew he would be busy later today as well as on the morrow; but first, his aim was to see the boys' mother.

While the two boys went in, Manfred stepped further out to greet the Earth Cleric. Mandred quickly related what concerned his wife, and what the local Hag had been giving her the past week. Earth Father nodded at each of the teas and herbal remedies that she had used. She appeared competent in the treatment of basic illnesses, though Manfred's description of Lililia's condition was indicative of some ailment more serious than that.

"No, no foul in any of those, sir," he said. "Your Hag knows a good bit of herbalism and general remedies. What she gave your wife would certainly not have hurt her, and likely helped in some ways. May I go in and see her?"

Manfred nodded. He was discouraged by how quickly his wife had slipped while the boys had been away. He blamed himself, because he had let them go on the hunt. He knew his wife was devoted to her sons and would miss their daily times together reading, singing, and talking about all they had done and learned. But the boys had been excited by the opportunity to hunt the big cat, and it was to be Jared's first time far afield without another grownup on the trek. Unfortunately, Lililia had taken a turn for the worse almost immediately. Two days later, he had the Hag visit; and, he had to admit, she had been able to reduce his wife's fever and ease her suffering.

As soon as he went in to see Lililia, Earth Father sent the boys from the room so he could examine their mother carefully. While he was ministering to her, the boys spent the time with Manfred going over their trek in great detail, particularly the entire preparation and hunt of the mountain lion. Manfred was pleased with all they had accomplished. Finally, they began the tale of their encounter with the bandits on the road back to Permis. Manfred could find no fault there either. The boys had reacted as he had trained them; and though he did not say so, they could tell he was satisfied with the choices they had made.

About a half hour later, Earth Father came out fingering his medallion and looking drained himself. Manfred drew him to the dining table near the warm stove; and with mugs of hot rum thinned with spring water, they talked while Lililia rested.

"She is fighting a bad canker in her liver. It has spread quite a bit, but I was able to halt its progress and reduce the size. Unfortunately, it has already done considerable damage. I do not know if one of my more powerful brethren could do more than I, but likely not. Unless we priests can catch a disease at an early stage, healing of many of the organs of the body is beyond our abilities. What is encouraging, and I will know more tomorrow or the next day, is how effective I have been in halting the worm's growth. I will look in each day I am here, and do another healing in two days. If it works, as I believe it will, I may be able to remove the canker altogether."

Earth Father stopped, took a draught from his mug, and wiped his brow. Catching Manfred's eye, he said firmly, "She is weak; and with the damage to the liver, she will never regain her full strength or energy. Most importantly, you must watch her carefully. Any new illness could be devastating; she might not be able to fight it off. I will talk with your Hag and recommend certain herbal teas that will help build her endurance and vitality as much as can be expected. I will also talk with her about other remedies to use should Lililia catch some new illness. With the information I give her, she will do as much as almost anyone can for your wife.

"Most importantly, you must protect her the best that you can from affronts to her system. Keep her warm in the cold and try to air out the rooms often. When the weather is amenable, let her rest outside. That in itself will be a good tonic. She should cover her face much of the time when with others, particularly if going to a public gathering or event. Yet I would recommend limiting these as much as possible, as they can be very tiring. Though we do not know a great deal about how illnesses spread, being cautious is a good approach. Still, it is best if she can see

51

other people singly or in small groups; that is good for the soul. Use your best judgement."

He looked at Jared and Ge-or, then back to Manfred. "You will all need to take on many of the household duties. Though she will want to do all she did before, it is best that she limit herself to the things she enjoys doing the most, so as to not tire her excessively. I have told her all of this and more. However, most patients want to continue their lives as normally as possible. Help her do that, while limiting as much as feasible what she tries to do on a daily basis. To a certain extent, she will understand that she now has limitations.

"One other thing – perhaps the most important – keep her spirits up. How we feel within is often reflected outwardly in our bodies. It is one of our order's prime teachings. All the things you do for each other, and with and for your mother, can make a difference.

"Any questions? Manfred? Boys?"

Though Jared and Ge-or could have asked dozens of questions, they deferred to Manfred. He had nodded at all that the good father had spoken about; and when the cleric had finished, he rose and went in to see his wife. Earth Father gestured for the boys to follow him outside.

"Is there a place we can talk privately?"

Ge-or nodded. He led the cleric around to a door that led out of the stockade near the village gardens. From there they went south, to the edge of the hills and onto another path leading into the rocky scape.

They stopped near an outcropping. "Thank you, Earth Father, for your help with our mother," Ge-or said. "We are sincerely grateful. You are welcome to stay with us, though there is a larger house near the square that often serves as an inn, renting to travelers. You would be more comfortable there; and there would be no charge, since you have offered to hold clinic. Understand that people here will make small contributions, as well, for your efforts on their behalf. Please accept them, for not to would be an insult."

"Yes, I have encountered that all along the coast here. The north country people are a sturdy lot, but kind to the bone. Thank you."

"Also," Ge-or added, "please plan to eat with us this eve, though others will offer as well. Mother will insist, and Jared and I will manage to make the gobbler more than edible with guidance from her. She is a good cook, and I know Father will insist, too, since you helped her so much."

Earth Father nodded. "One thing I should tell you both, that I did not wish your father to hear – your mother's illness will be difficult on him. He will blame himself for bringing her here – taking her from the safe haven of her home. In truth, there is no fault. They were in love, are in love, and love is the foundation for true living.

"Take care of your father, too. He may push you even harder because of what he takes upon himself regarding your mother. Her illness may weigh heavily on his shoulders; and he may, in different ways, take that out on you. Be patient with him if you can; help him when he allows you to."

Jared and Ge-or were quiet for several minutes as they walked further up the path. Though they understood in some ways what Earth Father had told them, it was hard to completely internalize what that would mean. Ge-or understood more than Jared that this cleric had given them much to ponder and discuss.

Suddenly Ge-or stopped. "Wait!" he hissed. He slipped behind a boulder, waving at Earth Father and Jared to do the same.

"Sh-h-h," he whispered. Ge-or pointed at a movement far up along the tree line that was moving sideways to the stiff breeze.

"Something up there," Jared whispered, "black against the sky, yet within the trees. Taller than a wolf, humanoid I would hazard. I can't imagine what else would be up here this time of day going crossways to the wind. Should we trail it?"

"Let's keep watch for a few minutes," Ge-or said.

"I think it may be our friends from the tavern," Earth Father whispered. "I have sensed something this afternoon that felt off. An oily shadow in my mind and chill in my body. I think they may have followed us… Ge-or?"

"Nay. I felt nothing; just noticed that odd movement in the trees. What could they want with us?".

53

"I know not. Perhaps simply revenge, a sense of duty to their betters, or to gather information, as I have been trying to do since I encountered them."

"Shouldn't we go after them?" Jared asked, again.

"Nay, I think not. Let us see if they stay around or slink away like the vermin they are. I need to go back and set up clinic with your village Hag. It is expected; and though I am tired, there is much I can do with the herbs, tinctures, and blessed essences I have with me."

"Let's keep our eye out the rest of today and tomorrow, Jared," Ge-or said. "If we see them again, we can talk with Father and see what he thinks. Come, Earth Father is right; we should return to the village and spend time with Mother."

It was after Jared and Ge-or helped their mother get dinner started that Jared brought out the old portative harp and showed it to her. It brought a bright smile to her face. "This is a fine instrument," she said, "though you will need to work hard to bring it back to life. I can tell you much about what to do. Once it is playable, I will teach you to play with the limited skills I have, though I never learned to read music, only to play by ear."

"I want to hear you play, Mother. We have always loved when you sing to us, especially when we were small. Perhaps we can sing duets together while I play."

Lililia dabbed at her eyes. She was joyed that her son had such a love of music. One of the things she had missed the most when deciding to leave Moulanes with Manfred was the incredible music the elven musicians improvised of an eve. Though her talents had been elsewhere, she had learned to play the lyre and harp a bit and had spent time with the luthiers during her formative years, learning what she could about instrument making by watching and asking questions.

"There is much to do, Jared. While you are fixing the damaged areas and replacing pegs, I will teach you to make strings. It is a difficult process because you need to dry, scrape, cut, and treat sheep's gut – finally, twisting the strands into different lengths and thicknesses to fit the instrument. It is a long, tedious process. If you want to play, it is something you will need to learn."

"I will do all you ask, Mother, if it will please you."

"It will please me more than you can know, my son. By the time we have it back to playing, I will have made you a protective covering for it from the cougar pelt. It will also please me to put it to such a use.

"One other thing, Jared. Remember that in your heart, music is a blessing that will speak to you throughout your life. Let it flow through you; use your talent to calm and heal when you and others have need of such. The music that sings in your heart has helped me more than anything for my loneliness from my kin. It was difficult for me to leave my heritage, my home, and my people; but because of my love for your father, and then for you boys, I would give it again a thousand-thousand more times.

"Music is who you are, sweet boy. Remember that." Lililia quieted then and closed her eyes. On a strong impulse from within, Jared softly began to sing a song that his mother had taught him – it was about green hills, lush pastures, and home.

After, Jared sat with her, humming soothing tunes that came to him as she rested. When she was fully asleep, he kissed her cheek gently, tears forming in his eyes. Gods willing, she will live long enough to see me grown, he thought.

It was later that evening, when Jared had gone to the workshop used by the village to begin cleaning the portative harp, and Manfred was making a last check on their animals, that Lililia asked Ge-or to come into the large bedroom. She was once again sitting in the rocking chair near the window, a warm woolen shawl about her shoulders. It was already starting to cool down quickly; and though Manfred had brought a foot warmer with coals from their stove for her, there was a chill settling in early that eve.

"Sit, Ge-or." Lililia pointed to the bed. "I have something I need to tell you before... Well, though the Earth cleric has healed the worst of my illness, I am greatly weakened; and I must prepare should I succumb to something sooner than later."

"Mother!"

"Be still, Ge-or. You are the eldest, and you must look after Jared and your father. You will need to be strong for both of them. Jared looks to you more than you might think. He will be devastated when I pass to the next world – or so the good cleric believes happens when we die. You must be a rock for your brother; he is a sensitive. If we have time, you, Manfred, and I will help him learn to be strong, resilient, vital. Push him when you must, but also, be kind. He will need that from you, for Manfred has difficulty showing such emotions."

Ge-or nodded at her words; everything she said he knew was true, though he could not have put it in words so readily himself.

"You must also watch yourself, my brave boy. Though you have great strength in you already, and will have more as you become a man, your heart is not unlike Jared's in many ways. What I have given you both, in my marriage to your father, is the kindness and compassion of my people. Remember this, for it will fare you well in your work with the peoples of Borea. I know that you are already restless. Soon enough, you will seek to know this world and those who dwell in it. Your brother will follow a different path."

Lililia quieted for a moment; then she reached out to take one of Ge-or's large hands in hers.

Though Ge-or was puzzled by what his mother had just said, he did not query her. He bowed his head and kissed the delicate hand that lay in his.

Finally, his mother spoke again. "There is something I wish you to have, my son. I will tell you of it today; but if I pass sooner, your father will keep it until you reach manhood. You have seen it hundreds of times, and probably not remarked on it."

As she spoke, Lililia slid her right hand over her left and began to twist a ring off of her middle finger. When she held it out toward Ge-or, he could see it was a simple thing. Set in white gold, maybe platinum, was a single stone – a medium sapphire perhaps. He took it gingerly in his hand. It felt warm, quite warm; he shifted it to his left.

"That is its aura – the warmth," she said. "Pay attention, Ge-or." Lililia caught his eye. Then, as if remembering something said long ago, she said, "Remember: a life for a life. Use it only if you must. Use it for love."

After another minute, Lililia held her hand out. Ge-or gave the ring back to her, watching as she put it on her left middle finger.

"It is what I was told upon the gifting – from my grandfather in parting – his only recognition of my leaving with your father. It will be yours, Ge-or, because I know now that I will never have a use for it. Use it wisely, my son, and know I love you. Don't forget what I said, 'Remember: a life for a life. Use it only if you must. Use it for love.' It is all he said to me; all I know about it."

Ge-or bowed his head.

***

The two days that Earth Father stayed in Thiele were a blessing to the villagers, and especially to Ge-or and Jared. Though an initiate, he had a powerful healing gift; and the Earth Father had seen anyone who had needed help, including many who came in from the surrounding countryside. He had also seen Lililia several more times, making sure she was in the best of health by the time he prepared to set off.

Many in the village came to see him out the west gate. He had helped so many, and his demeanor was so affable, that they were sad to see him go. As it was in the north country, the villagers had provided him with many gifts of food and other useful items, including gloves, scarves, hats, socks, as well as odds and ends useful for a long trek. Dumpy looked overloaded and a bit forlorn as they headed to the south, though the people of Thiele had even thought to gift several bags full of oats and other grains for his nosebag.

Jared and Ge-or had asked permission of their father to go as far as the top of the first ridge to see him safely off. The boys were sad to see the loquacious cleric leave. Though he had often gibed them about this and that, and appeared to chat about relatively innocuous topics, they both knew that he had given them a great deal to think about. He would make a good priest, for he knew what to say and how to say it so that they would consider his words for some time, learning from the true purpose and meaning he had imparted.

With hugs and final goodbyes said, and a last carrot for Dumpy, the boys turned and headed back down the path. There was work in the fields – readying them for the spring – and weapons practice, all before dinner. They waved one more time, as the Earth Cleric crested the rise and disappeared into the spruce beyond.

"I think we will be lonely for a while, brother," Jared mused.

"We have already been lonely for a while," Ge-or said. "As half-elven, he showed us that."

"Truly, I have been thinking on it." Jared quieted for a moment, then asked, "You know that Earth Father spoke with Father about us, as well as Mother?"

Jared laughed, "Aye, and he said Manfred was not much of a conversationalist."

"True," Ge-or grinned. "

Jared nodded thoughtfully. "They both seem lighter and, well, more affectionate too. Like some burden has been lifted from them.

"Mayhap, Father will let us have more freedom to explore the world now, if we ask.".

"We are both still young, Jared."

"And not."

"Aye, and not."

They walked on quietly for a while. When Ge-or spoke again, he was a bit more pensive. "There is still much to learn, brother. You have your lute now and will have lessons from Mother soon. And remember, you start with the blacksmith this fall. Father wants us both to start studying tactics, war machinery, even lance training; those will keep us busy.

"Did I tell you he plans to get a horse, maybe two this year? That is, if the crops are good."

"Truly?" Jared asked, intrigued. Both the boys were now too big to ride on Nelly, and they had long yearned to gallop about in the saddle pretending they were knights a-horse. Still, they both also understood that the animals would be for farm purposes, not for two boys to galivant about imagining grand adventures.

"Aye."

"Then, as you said, we will be busy."

Ge-or nodded.

The boys quieted again as they entered the upper fields. A few minutes later, Ge-or clapped Jared on his shoulder. "I was thinking on that last quest we had planned," he offered.

"The one with the three-headed dragon and the TWO beautiful maidens at the end?"

Ge-or laughed, "Aye."

"I want to save the dark-haired one." Jared laughed too. "Where were we?"

"I believe I had just killed the great ogre, and you were trying to fight a nasty troll."

"Trying?"

After all boys, will be boys...

Dark of the Moon
Three days later

A dark figure steps out from the stand of tall spruce. Two others, behind and to his left as befit their rank, come out at the same time.

The lone man, tall, thin, with a hawk-like nose, is wearing a thin black cassock, though it is still quite brisk this night. He likes the cold.

There is something else — it seems to radiate from him and it speaks of evil. Perhaps it is his visage — sharp, penetrating, icy, vicious. There is no softness in it; no kindness or generosity; nothing that suggests his humanity except that he seems a man; yet his form is incomprehensively darker than the darkness encircling him. Even when he looks back toward his comrades — one a huge man bristling with weapons, dressed completely in black leather; the other a small, weaselly acolyte, black-robed, hooded — there is no kindness, or even recognition, just a snarl of disgust.

Turning back, and still not able to fully see what he wants, he steps up on a flat stone, looking down the ridge toward the last village set along the northwest coast of Borea. From this new perch, the priest can see the whole stockade.

He smiles a harsh smile — almost a death grin, should anyone have seen it. Thiele was too soft a name for such a place. Soon enough, he would rename it — Infernata — Death from Fire.

A few of the houses still have a light or two interrupting the full blackness of the town's outline. Aberon is more comfortable in darkness. He has cloaked himself magically in its protective web and chosen this night of no moon; so he can gloat without that dread orb hanging overhead. Still, it is the season for falling stars, the brief flashes across the sky annoying.

After a few minutes studying the town, he takes a small object from his pocket. He briefly rubs the rondelle between his fingers. It is a carved piece, worn virtually smooth in places by such caressing, though now there is no power remaining in it. He holds the wood medallion forward – a device that looks to be a wreath with a cross of twigs and a tiny gem centered in its middle. Childish. He holds it out further; and with a grip enhanced by inner force, he crushes it easily in his hand, letting the pieces fall to the rock. He kicks at the fragments, then blows the remaining dust from his hands.

Holding the small garnet up between his fingers, he examines the dusky red stone with his own power. It had not fared its owner well, he smirks. A pitifully weak stone, of no use to him or his brethren, he flicks it into the darkness. Then Aberon returns to his contemplation of the scene below.

Some day he would return to this place and see the end of the town below. There was something here that he wanted, needed, if he was to impress his overseers, the Black Druids. For now, Aberon had more important things to do.

He spits toward the town; then turns around.

As he turns, the briefest flash of a falling star catches the Dark Priest's forehead, illuminating the blood painted there – the hunter's mark.

Excerpt from Book I

of

The Chronicles of Borea

The Making of a Bard

Preludio

Joseph E. Koob II

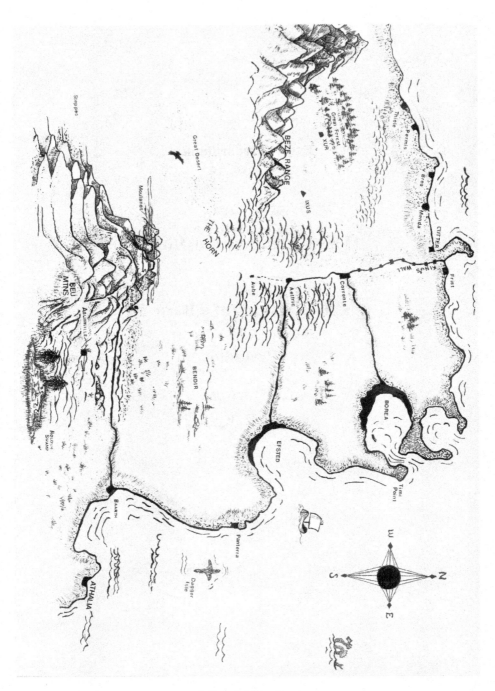

Map of Borea

NOTE

The Hunter's Mark takes place several years before **The Chronicles of Borea** -- a seven-book Sword & Sorcery Fantasy. **The Hunter's Mark** was written after the series was completed, and is a stand-alone Novella. It can serve as a Prequel to the series, or it can be read as an independent short work.

Death in the West

"Kla-a-ng, Kla-a-ng!" The deep pitch resound of the village bell echoed across the scattered boulders of the high hills. The heads of the two hunters came up at the first peal. The older lad slung his bounty of coneys over his shoulder and shouted, "Come on, Jared, the boats must have come early." Broad of shoulder, he grinned at his younger brother and then took off with an easy trot down the slope toward the stockade. However, by the time they neared the narrow path that led through the rock outcropping between them and the village, the younger lad, almost as tall as his brother and more lightly built, passed him.

The bell continued ringing, and as they hurried through the twisting route to the pasture above the town, Jared glanced behind him and gasped out, "Something must be wrong, Ge-or. Hurry!"

They came around the last bend in the path and slid to a halt on an overhang that led down to the lower fields of barley and oats. In an instant, they took in the implausible scene below. Jared yelled again, "Qa-ryks!" Dropping his rabbits, he plunged down toward the stockade. His brother followed several steps behind, both unslinging their short hunting bows as they ran.

From their vantage point above, they could see that the western stockade wall had been breached in several places. Gaping holes, blasted in the sturdy logs by some immense force, were filled with the struggling of men and large beasts as the villagers strove to stem the attack of the marauders. Inside the town's perimeter, old men, women, and even children were trying to erect a secondary line of defense around the buildings that fronted the town square. The whole scene was a frenzy. Many villagers fought fiercely with whatever they had been able to bring to the battle: short swords, axes, heavy hammers, as well as pitchforks, hoes, and other farming implements. They were keeping the onslaught at bay, while others piled carts, rugged hand-hewn furniture, and miscellaneous crates up into a makeshift barrier at the center of the hamlet.

As they broke into a sprint, the brothers were more than three-hundred paces from the closest attack point. Jared ran at full speed, using the downward slope to gain even more momentum and distance with each long stride. He was soon far ahead of his brother. As he neared the log wall of the outer fortifications, he could see that the battle had moved inward toward the heart of the village. Running toward the nearest breach, he could now see the charred logs and hot coals from the blast that had leveled a good part of the wall. Moving quickly north to gain access, he was about to step through the opening toward the noise of the fighting when his brother gasped out from behind, "Wait, we'll get better shots from the roofs." Jared spun around and waved, waiting for Ge-or to come up. Keeping watch for any beasts that might head their way, he held his bow at the ready with one of his hunting arrows nocked.

From where he stood, Jared could see the devastation of the initial attack. Bodies of both men and Qa-ryks lay in contorted positions along the fiery path. The eight-foot-high stockade had been struck by some mysterious power, which had burnt a twenty-foot-wide section of the heavy logs. Several houses inside the wall had also caught fire from the intensity of the blast. These were also burning fiercely, and other nearby buildings were smoking from the heat. The close proximity of the houses in the mountain hamlet, built to help withstand the ravages of fierce winter snows and cold winds from the sea, made fire a threat to the whole village. Though the townspeople were always prepared to fight a fire, this was no ordinary blaze.

As soon as Ge-or reached Jared, the two young men ran to the east along the inside of the stockade wall until they came to a dwelling that was untouched by flames. Replacing his bow over his neck and shoulder in order to give his brother a boost, Jared helped hoist Ge-or up onto the roof.

Once Ge-or was perched precariously on the steep slant of the rough wooden shingles, he reached down to give his brother a hand. As Jared began to climb, a Qa-ryk appeared from around the building to the north. Ge-or drew back and yelled, "Look out!"

Jared instinctively pushed off from the logs, rolling to the side as he hit the ground. Not having time to retrieve his bow from his back, he drew his hunting knife from the sheath on his belt as he came to rest on his knees.

The Qa-ryk, wielding a wicked double-bladed axe in one claw, rushed at him, roaring. Ge-or, above, had nocked an arrow and was drawing back as the broad blade began to descend toward Jared's head. The younger lad, warrior-trained, crouched ready to jump clear of the blow.

The arrow from above struck the hairy beast in the back of its thick neck, causing the stroke of the axe to go wide. The Qa-ryk reared back; and Jared, using the opening, lunged forward, driving his knife deep into the creature's gut. Ripping it sideways, he withdrew the sharp blade in a gruesome swath through its stomach and intestines. Mortally wounded, the powerful beast was still able to reach out and claw at Jared as it fell away from the knife in its gut. The four-inch-long nails of its left claw ripped across the top back of the boy's light leather jerkin and right shoulder. A second arrow from Ge-or struck the Qa-ryk in the center of its chest, and the enemy warrior swayed for a moment before falling back, full-length in the dirt.

Jared, having spun to the side, began to straighten when his brother yelled from his perch on the edge of the roof, "Are you all right?"

"I guess I'll manage," Jared answered. He could feel blood leaking from the wound, but it did not hurt any more than if he had been hit with a heavy punch. "He caught me in the shoulder. It's not bad. Give me a second to stop the bleeding."

"Get the arrows; we'll need them," Ge-or shouted.

Trying to focus in spite of the flash of pain that hit him as he moved, Jared ripped a length of cloth from his woolen cloak. Working quickly, he managed to staunch the flow of blood with a hastily tied bandage.

Bending over the dead creature, Jared began to cut out the two arrows. He was seeing one of these massive humanoids close-up for the first time in his life, yet he had butchered many a big game animal; and since the anatomy of all mammalian creatures is similar, he made quick work of the grisly task. Cutting quickly through red flesh and sinew, he reached the carefully crafted steel arrow heads and drew them out.

The beast was heavily muscled and a foot taller than Jared. It had sparse, short, coarse, brownish-red hair on its body and limbs. On the nails of one of its clawed hands, Jared could see the red crimson of his own blood and several clots of pink flesh. He swallowed hard, pushing down the threat of nausea at the sight.

Though its features were twisted in death, Jared noted the heavy jaw, sloping forehead, deep, close-set eyes, and long upper fangs that curved slightly in toward its chin, all of which gave the beast its fearsome visage. Until this attack, Qa-ryks had never been this far north to threaten the Borean seacoast hamlets. Jared and Ge-or's only exposure to them had been on long treks to the south and west during trapping parties with their father into the Dark Forest. They had always given the beasts wide berth when they had seen them.

A hissed, "Hurry!" from above brought Jared back to the immediacy of the task at hand. Dismissing the heavy battle-axe as too cumbersome for either of them to wield, Jared turned back toward the building and began to climb.

A minute later, with Ge-or's help, Jared was on the roof. He handed an arrow to his brother. "The one in his neck broke when he fell. I cut out the arrowhead."

"The axe?"

"Too big even for you to handle, Ge-or. Come on, let's go." Both boys turned and scrambled quickly up the slope of the roof.

When they reached its high peak, they could see that the battle was now focused in the center of the village. Running down the far slope of the roof, each, in turn, leapt across the four-foot distance to the next roof. Ge-or led the way. They had to leap across several more roofs before the beasts were in range of their shortbows, ending up perched on the edge of a small house at the far southwest of the square.

The smoke from burning houses drifted all around them. It was difficult, even from their vantage point, to get a good perspective of the state of the battle. The fighting was fiercest in the northwest corner of the newly fortified square, where the major Qa-ryk thrust was aimed. Many of the beasts were crowding together, trying to smash their way through the hastily formed barricade to get at the villagers. Even the older women and young lads were fighting now. The din of the battle was a deafening, continuous roar -- the beasts' guttural battle cries mixing with the clanging of weapons and the frantic shouts and screams of the defenders.

The two lads stood on the north slope of the roof and nocked arrows to their bows trying to pick out targets within range. They shot carefully, aiming to wound each beast they hit badly enough so it would be out of the fighting. Their hunting arrows and light shortbows, while meticulously designed and formed under the watchful eye of their father, were intended for small animals, rabbits and squirrels, and the occasional deer. They were not powerful enough to bring down a Qa-ryk warrior unless the shot was extremely accurate. Though both boys were excellent marksmen, capable of skewering a running rabbit at thirty paces, the swirling smoke and decreasing light made it difficult for them to find targets.

Jared, the better marksman, caught one big Qa-ryk neatly in the eye with his first shot. The creature straightened, stiffened, and pitched backward, dead before it hit the ground. Ge-or's first shot stuck deep in the neck of one beast who was trying to claw up a sturdy oaken chest to get at two women fending it off with pitchforks. The beast grabbed at its throat, collapsing backward as the two pitchforks stabbed into its chest.

The two boys continued shooting – picking off the closest beasts with carefully placed shots. Unfortunately, it took only a few minutes for them to use up most of their small supply of arrows. Finally, Ge-or stood, handing his last three shafts to his brother. "Here!" he shouted above the din, "we've got to get more arrows and our swords. Stay as long as you can, then head back over the roofs to our house. I'll meet you on my way back. Watch out! If they see you, they might still have buoas. Good luck." Ge-or clapped his brother on his unbandaged shoulder; then he ran to the side of the roof and leapt across to the next dwelling to the east.

Jared, swinging back around, loosed his arrow as it came to bear on the first vital point he focused on – the ear of a beast trying to push through a breach in the defenses. The shaft hit dead-center and penetrated about half-way into the beast's brain; the Qa-ryk thrashed wildly as he fell. Jared caught a loose nail with his boot, causing his next shot to go a bit wide, hitting the Qa-ryk he had seen sneaking around the house below him in its shoulder, just above the heart. The beast roared in pain and ducked back around the building.

Swearing at the less-than-perfect shot, Jared nocked another arrow and searched through the smoke for a target. Suddenly, a gust of wind blew the dark gray haze from the square, and he caught a glimpse of the whole battle. He immediately realized how hopeless the situation truly was. A large company of the monstrous beasts had attacked their village; the entire square was now surrounded. Though the villagers were putting up a stalwart defense, they were over-matched; and there was no place to which they could retreat. The beasts had surrounded the makeshift barricade; and already several had clawed their way through the obstacles before them, engaging the defenders within the village center. Jared's and Ge-or's fine shooting had slowed the breakthrough in this quarter; unfortunately, most of their fellow villagers were not trained fighters.

Jared knew that there was something terribly wrong about this whole scene. Qa-ryks roved in small bands, seldom more than ten or twelve in a group. Even a clan was rarely more than twenty-five or thirty of the beasts. That was why the mountain villages, though settled near the eastern part of the Qa-ryk range, were considered safe from attack. Their only concern with the beasts was when hunting or trapping teams were out far from their protective stockade. These groups could be vulnerable to being ambushed. From what he could see, their village had been assaulted by over a hundred of the fierce warriors; the two hundred inhabitants, only a third men and women of fighting age, didn't stand a chance.

Even so, the resistance was determined. A bright flash of light, rising above one part of the beleaguered square, caught his eye. Jared immediately recognized the flaming blue arc of an elven sword rising again and again above the fray. He knew that his father – one of the best weapons-men of the early Qa-ryk Wars – was leading the defense at that point. There, the men and women were holding back the worst of the attack.

Jared took heart and resolved to move in closer to the melee to make sure his five remaining arrows counted. He leapt across several roofs before bracing for another shot.

Suddenly, the sky darkened, as if night had descended instantaneously instead of waiting for the twilight to progress further. A rush of wind accompanied the blackness as a massive form swept down from above toward the northwest corner of the square. For an instant, the fighting stopped throughout the whole village. The Qa-ryks broke off their attack and backed hastily from the crude fortifications.

A second later, a huge belch of flame came from the huge beast's open maw as it swept down close above the square. The blast of flame roiled out, engulfing the center of the defense. The bravely wielded blue sword, caught in the center of the liquid fire, faltered in its highest arc and fell.

That was all the boy saw, because the smoke from the new blazes and the tears streaming from his eyes obscured the rest. Now he knew what magic the Qa-ryks had used to breach the village walls. However inconceivable it was, the normally reclusive beasts had somehow enlisted the aid of a red dragon. The horrific winged creature had destroyed the last serious defense in one fiery blast; with a bellowing roar, it turned neatly on its tail and flew off into the west.

The burst of intense fire from the red dragon changed the whole scene from one of willful resistance to a complete rout and massacre. Qa-ryks renewed their assault and streamed into the square from all sides, cutting down men, women, and children as they charged inward. Those villagers that could get away, ran toward the eastern gate. Their last hope was to out-distance the lumbering beasts. Most, however, were met and brutally torn apart by long claws and sharp fangs.

Jared, fighting back tears, kept shooting. He was nocking his next-to-last arrow when one of the beasts espied him on the roof. Just in time, he saw the flick of the beast's wrist, and he dove backwards and to the side. An instant later, a wicked spiral blade buried itself in the wood shingles only inches to the right and above his forehead. Getting up quickly, Jared ran further up the slope trying to reset his arrow. As he was setting up for a shot, he looked down and saw the beast bringing his arm up to throw again. Knowing his shortbow and hunting arrow were no match for the deadly buoa thrown by an experienced warrior, he judiciously scampered over the peak of the roof. Running as fast as he could on the shingles, he headed toward the southeast corner and leapt for the next roof. He had to find his brother.

Roof followed roof as he ran to the east. The steep slopes were hazardous and made of rough-hewn slats; nonetheless, Jared's half-elf agility gave him a distinct advantage. He was as sure-footed as any. He and his brother had often played games scampering up and down the steep roofs while practicing their swordplay. He would be able to outdistance the slower Qa-ryk, but not by much.

At one point he caught a glimpse of the big beast still following him, though he lost sight of it as he ran over another peak. Jared was now more concerned with the fate of his brother than for himself. Ge-or would need to know what had happened in the square. As he neared their house, he shouted his brother's name. He got no reply.

The last house before his own was burning brightly, so when Jared reached the edge of the roof he knelt down, grasped the eave, and spun over the edge, dropping lightly to the ground. Running past the burning dwelling, he finally caught sight of Ge-or. His brother was standing in front of their log house fighting, keeping two of the dread beasts at bay with his sword. One dead Qa-ryk lay at his feet. He could see that Ge-or was bleeding from several superficial claw wounds, yet he seemed to be holding his own.

Ge-or was a remarkable swordsman; nevertheless, in the close confines between houses, and pressed by two of the heavy beasts, he was giving ground slowly. Jared knew his brother was waiting for the right opening to gut the foremost beast, but he also knew they had little time before other Qa-ryks would be upon them. Their house, which Ge-or was backing toward, was also beginning to smoke.

As he moved forward, Jared brought up his bow, drawing back as he raised it. When his aim came to bear, he let it fly into the back of the nearest Qa-ryk's neck. The arrow struck the beast, penetrating deeply, just as Ge-or parried a swipe from the foremost beast. Flipping the blade under the creature's arm, Ge-or plunged it deep into its upper belly. At that moment, another Qa-ryk appeared from the left and swung at Ge-or with a massive cudgel. Dodging under an attack by the beast that Jared had shot, Ge-or saw the swipe coming an instant too late. The heavy club struck Ge-or's temple with a loud sickening thwack. Jared saw his brother sink slowly to his knees, falling face-forward onto the packed earth.

Readying his last arrow for a shot, Jared caught sight of the Qa-ryk that had been chasing him as it came between the houses to his right. Seeing the buoa in its claw, he changed his mind and tried to get past the one with the club. He ducked forward, running as fast as he could toward Ge-or's crumbled form. Reacting on pure instinct, he grabbed the quiver of arrows from his brother's back as he passed, ripping upward until the leather strap broke; then he swung into the open doorway of their smoking home. Dashing through the large main room to the back, he flung himself at the window, closing his eyes tightly as he smashed through one of the few luxuries they had owned – a glass window his father had purchased for his elven wife. Landing on his side, he rolled to his feet and raced to the left past another flaming house.

The whole village was afire now; Jared had no choice but to flee. He had watched his father die in an instant from the dragon's fiery breath, and now saw his brother felled by a Qa-ryk club. With a massive beast following, the burning anguish in his chest would have to wait. Tears blurring his vision, he ran alongside the stockade wall, hoping that some of the villagers had managed to get to the eastern gate and safely onto the road to Permis. Once on the road, they might be able to outdistance the heavy-legged Qa-ryks. With luck, they could make it to the next town to warn their neighbors. Having only a quiver of arrows and a hunting knife, Jared knew he was of little consequence to what remained of the battle.

Crying bitterly, he made his way as fast as he could to a small door in the southern wall of the stockade. Ahead, he could see other beasts rushing toward the eastern gate, but no other villagers were in sight. Opening the door, he stepped through, glancing back once again to see if there were any others who might make it out that way. When he looked left, he saw the large Qa-ryk with the buoa come around the corner of the nearest house. Jared immediately slammed the heavy panel shut behind him. Searching the area around the door, he found a small log, which he wedged up against the heavy panel. Finally, he turned and ran for the hills to the south and east.

Jared was tired. A three-hour weapons training session early that morning with their father, as well as the day's work helping with the harvest in the fields, had taken a toll; and the early evening hunting trip up in the hills with his brother had taxed him further. He was, however, young and able. The swirl of emotions tightening his chest helped him make good time up the rocky slope. At first, he didn't think about where he was going; he went up and away, trying to put some distance between him and the beast that was trailing. As his jumbled thoughts began to settle and his grief subsided into a slow-burning rage, he oriented himself along a well-worn path due south, that went up into the hills.

Jared had no doubt the Qa-ryk was tracking him. From what his father had taught him, he knew they did not give up on fugitives readily. As a half-elf, he would be a special prize this far to the north. If he were taken alive, he would be tortured mercilessly for days. He was not going to let that happen.

He was too far from the eastern road to cut over easily; still, he figured that if he got high enough into the hills and either outpaced or killed the Qa-ryk, he could wend his way back to help any who might have gotten free from the fighting. He knew this terrain well. He had spent his youth moving in and out of the many nooks and crannies of the rocky slopes on adventures with his brother. He and Ge-or often began their hunting expeditions heading up this very path.

He began to think more clearly and to formulate a tentative plan as he loped easily along the pebbly dirt path through the rocky terrain. After ten minutes, when the rocks began to get larger and more difficult to maneuver around and the path narrowed considerably, Jared struck off to the west. This was as good a place as he would find to set an ambush. The large brute would have trouble maneuvering on the narrow path, and the boulders would give Jared enough cover to get off one clean shot before the beast could spot him. If he was accurate, he might survive.

Two minutes later found Jared crouching on a small ledge in a natural hollow formed by two large boulders. This spot had been his secret hideaway for many years. It was a place where he had been able to think, read, and make up tunes while accompanying himself on his small portative harp. He always carried it on his back, even when hunting, for he never knew when a new tune might come to him.

As he waited in the increasing dark for the Qa-ryk, Jared reached back underneath his cloak to touch the strings and rosewood frame through the well-used cougar-pelt carry case his mother had made for it. Though he always felt the weight of the instrument on his back, it was reassuring to feel the light tension of the strings. With a deep sigh, he wondered if he would ever feel like singing again.

Turning his attention to his bow, he eased an arrow from the quiver. Nocking it, he pulled back slightly on the string, feeling the tension of the wood in his left hand. He prayed that his aim would be true for this one chance, because that would be all he would get. If he missed his aiming point, the beast would be on him in a second. He wished he had picked up Ge-or's sword; but in his frenzy to get away from the Qa-ryk, he barely had time to get the quiver.

Jared sensed the Qa-ryk's approach a moment before he heard scraping noises amongst the rocks. He drew back the bow string, relishing the feeling of resistance of the tightly-wound, carefully waxed gut. He waited. The large warrior became aware of Jared a split second after he came around the boulder; that instant cost him his life. Jared smoothly released the arrow at the yellowish gleam of the beast's left eye. Dropping the bow before he knew whether the arrow had hit where he had aimed, he vaulted up and back over the boulder behind him, drawing his hunting knife as he prepared for what might happen next.

A roar greeted the night air, convincing Jared that he had been true to his mark. Teetering on its heavy legs, it fell forward, the arrow protruding from its left eye socket. The beast was likely dead before it hit the ground; Jared wanted to be certain. He slid sideways around two boulders to come up behind it, lifted its heavy head, and slit its throat. The creature did not move; the arrow had penetrated into its brain.

As Jared stood over the fallen Qa-ryk, he saw that the creature was one of the ranking clan members. It was dressed in a chain mail shirt never found on their regular soldiers, and it had an ornate two-handed sword in its left claw. He stooped over the eight-foot body of the humanoid and began to search the corpse.

First, he drew out the beast's long hunting knife from its leather sheath. Small for a creature of this size, the blade would serve as a sword for Jared. Cutting out his arrow next, he returned it to his quiver.

Thankfully, the wood had held and not snapped when the beast fell. Finally, he cut off the Qa-ryk's food pouch, which he re-tied over his shoulder. Slipping the long knife into his own belt, he bent over and picked up the remaining buoa from the dead creature's claw. He handled the wicked spiral throwing blade gingerly, deciding at the last to place it in the large food pouch in between the dried meat and bread he found there.

Stepping back from the body, Jared closed his eyes and whispered a thank you to the gods. He was on his own now and would need to survive in the hills for at least a few days. Making a decision, he stepped toward the dead beast again and bent to search the body for a purse, eventually finding a small one tied around its belt. Jared cut it loose with his hunting knife and tied it to his own belt. He knew he would need everything he could find that might prove of any use. Thiele was destroyed, his family members and friends killed. He did not know if he would be able to go back to salvage anything within the next few days… or if he would ever wish to.

As he was about to leave, he noticed a large, irregularly shaped stone, bound by some light-colored metal, hanging from a leather thong around the beast's neck. Bending over, he cut the cord. Without looking at it, he tied it around his own neck to examine later. If it had any value, he might be able to trade it for supplies. He left the beast for the crows or its comrades to find and headed back to the southerly path, thence, further up into the high hills.

Brief Synopsis

The Chronicles of Borea, Book I, The Making of a Bard -- Preludio;
A Grand Epic Sword and Sorcery Fantasy, by Joseph E Koob II

A brutal attack by savage beasts and a red dragon sets three young
people on unforeseen paths where they begin to realize their diverse
talents – **Music**, **Might**, and **Magic**. Jared, a naturally talented musician
who is badly wounded in the massacre, fights his way into the hills
where he links up with Thistle, a young girl whose hidden magical
power both aids and threatens their survival. Meanwhile, Jared's
brother, Ge-or, an exceptionally trained warrior, is rescued by an
itinerant cleric whose efforts to save the town have been thwarted by
the evil Black Druid, Aberon, the ambitious dark priest who planned the
village's annihilation.

Using their abilities and training in unexpected ways to survive in the
wilds of Borea, these three young people set forth to avenge the deaths
of their friends and relatives. Yet Aberon remains on their trail while
planning a new attack that will destroy the last vestige of the
Kingdom's forces in the west, with them caught in his web.

Music:

A young half-elven lad discovers that the power of music influences his
direction in life.

"From the heart, Jared. It will vibrate when you have it right... ' He took
the little melody and began to twist it as only he could, blending the old
with the new until he was playing an intricate weave of the melody
amongst itself, supported by the most ethereal harmonies he had ever
played...

Might:

His brother, an exceptionally trained warrior, seeks vengeance on the
dragon that destroyed his village.

With both feet planted firmly on solid ground, he wove an intricate pattern with his blade, cleaving through the weapons, guards, flesh, and sinew of the beasts as they came at him. If the destruction of life could be considered an art, a type of beauty, it was certainly represented in how Ge-or handled his sword...

Magic:

The young girl's misuse of her hidden power shows that she needs to understand the most fundamental aspects of elemental magic before she destroys herself and others.

"At least, we know that you have been aware of the sensation of power before. All of that power, that sensation, Thistle, is your core energy. Once you can focus it to your center and are able to release or not release it at will, you will have made tremendous progress."

The series is a sweeping fantasy with intriguing plot twists interwoven in a moving fabric of a sensual and powerful writing style. A tale in the true sense of the word -- fun to read and captivating from one book to the next.

All Seven Books of **The Chronicles of Borea** series can be purchased at Amazon.com

Made in the USA
Columbia, SC
26 May 2023

16951404R10046